R of the Lost Gold

Riddle of the Lost Gold

by
Joan K. McAfee

SUNFLOWER UNIVERSITY PRESS.
1531 Yuma • P.O. Box 1009 • Manhattan, Kansas 66505-1009 USA

© 2002 Joan K. McAfee
Printed in the United States of America on acid-free paper.

Cover by Rod Hoover, St. George, Kansas.

ISBN 0-89745-262-3

Sunflower University Press is a wholly-owned subsidiary
of the non-profit 501(c)3 Journal of the West, Inc.

The fortress sleeps.
The hands at five, due west . . . .
Earth that welcomes gold returned to home.

Contents

Author's Preface	ix
Acknowledgments	xvii
Chapter One	
Unclaimed for a Hundred Years	1
Chapter Two	
A Good Campaigner	15
Chapter Three	
The House on Officers Row	18
Chapter Four	
The Siren Song of Gold	25
Chapter Five	
Farewell to Clear Creek Canyon	45
Chapter Six	
Old Granger and the Smoky Hill Trail	55
Chapter Seven	
Biding Time	71

Chapter Eight
　　Much to Think About　　　　　　　　　　74

Chapter Nine
　　Bad News　　　　　　　　　　　　　　78

Chapter Ten
　　All in a Day's Work　　　　　　　　　81

Chapter Eleven
　　Back to an Age Long Gone　　　　　　84

Chapter Twelve
　　Cheyenne Wells Station　　　　　　　86

Chapter Thirteen
　　Fort Wallace　　　　　　　　　　　　99

Chapter Fourteen
　　Custer and the Seventh Cavalry　　　111

Chapter Fifteen
　　The Trek to Fort Hays　　　　　　　114

Chapter Sixteen
　　Gold Returned to Home　　　　　　125

Chapter Seventeen
　　Yvette's Riddle　　　　　　　　　　128

Chapter Eighteen
　　How Perfectly Logical!　　　　　　　141

Chapter Nineteen
　　Thanks to Old Major　　　　　　　　145

Chapter Twenty
　　Facing the Vietnam War　　　　　　152

Chapter Twenty-One
　　Home from the War　　　　　　　　156

Selected Reading　　　　　　　　　　　　　162

Author's Preface

THE INSPIRATION FOR *Riddle of the Lost Gold* came from the bits and pieces of my recollections of Kansas and Colorado that I had acquired from living in those two states. My interest in their histories ultimately fit together as segments in my mind, forming a mental image of the rugged, adventurous, pioneer life in the mid-1800s. These histories subsequently, one hundred years later, met up with life in Kansas during the era of the Vietnam War, confirming once again that our present is always affected by our past.

When I was a small child in the mid-1930s, my father often took me with him on his walks along Big Creek, a stream only a "stone's throw" from our family home in Hays, Kansas. To

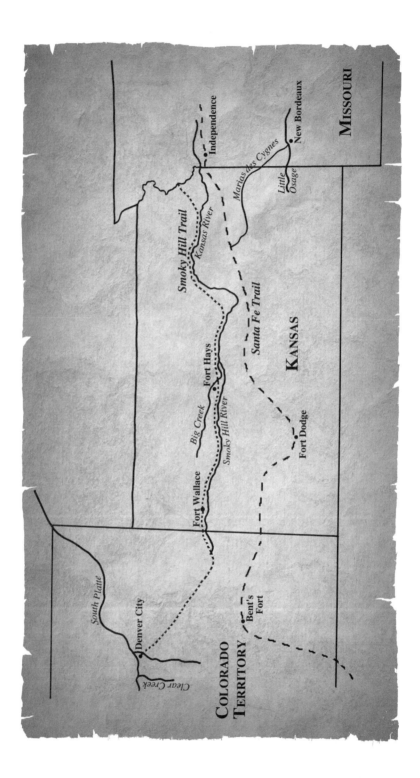

Author's Preface

the south, on the far side of Big Creek, was Fort Hays, a pioneer Kansas military post, a temporary stopping point for Lieutenant Colonel George A. Custer, and home of the famed Seventh Cavalry.

The Fort had been abandoned as an active military post since 1889. The blockhouse and the guardhouse had been left to the mercies of the elements, and the wooden houses on Officers Row had been torn down or moved into the town. The blockhouse that had served the Seventh Cavalry as Post Headquarters and the guardhouse, which was not only a jail but also a storage place for military munitions, were both built of ochre limestone, the almost indestructible building material used by early settlers of the region. Much labor would have been required to demolish those two buildings, so they had been left behind, forlorn reminders of the bloody years when they existed to help the U.S. Army contain the Indian Wars and bring a peaceful settlement to the region.

I recall one hot summer day in 1936. Our walk had ended at the guardhouse and I was playing in the tiny jail cells along the west wall, all the while listening to the low moan of the Kansas wind as it wandered in and out through the empty building. I was only five years old, yet even then it occurred to me that at some point the structure where I was happily passing time had been habited by people who were long dead. I asked my father who they were, and he briefly told me about the Seventh Cavalry. Then he remarked, "Also, Custer was here." But as my father seldom imparted the knowledge he had taken in over a lifetime of constant reading, I was left to ask myself, "Who was Custer?"

It took me many years to acquire a modicum of insight into the complex character that was George Armstrong Custer. In reading about America's Civil War, I came across accounts of his battle stratagems and comments about his heroism. And I found him mentioned when I read the Civil War journals written by private citizens. (A Southern lady thought he was "intriguing"; he had shared with her a picture of his beautiful wife Libby.) I also read Elizabeth (Libby) Custer's books and *Custer, Come at Once*, by local Hays, Kansas, historian Father Blaine Burkey.

In a wider sense, *The Queen City: A History of Denver*, by Lyle A. Dorsett and Michael McCarthy, increased my understanding of how America's fledgling Western towns grew. Through this book I was introduced to Denver's early influential citizens: William N. Byers, who had printed Denver's first newspaper; General William Larimer, who had founded the town in 1858; and Luther Kountze, the banker.

In 1963, as a young married woman, I moved to Arvada, a suburb of Denver. Each day on my way to work I crossed over a small bridge that spanned a mountain stream meandering through the helter-skelter sprawl of Arvada's small businesses and its concrete and asphalt streets. The stream was Clear Creek, a misnomer at the time, for it was bank-full of foam from effluent containing non-biodegradable laundry detergent. Where I lived, Clear Creek was anything but clear!

On numerous Sundays after church, my husband and I took our children on day trips through Clear Creek Canyon, wending our way up the hairpin curves on the narrow roadway beside the creek's fast-flowing streambed to the roadside parks just below the timberline, where we usually stopped for a picnic. Once again I found myself listening to the wind, this time moaning in the topmost branches of the tall pines. I came to know Clear Creek Canyon, although I do not recall ever venturing down the south fork of Clear Creek where on January 6th, 1859, young George Jackson had discovered gold. In the *Time-Life* series of *The Old West*, I came across an account of his momentous discovery. The hot mineral springs located near Clear Creek had mountain sheep that came to graze in the green grass where hot vapors had melted the snow. While at the springs, Jackson killed a buck and fed chops to himself and his two dogs.

Thus came to my imaginary world the characters of the *Riddle of the Lost Gold* — Pierre Prideaux, Anton Dumler, Pride, and faithful Bruno.

Over the years, I also have been an avid reader of the pioneer journals that were left to posterity by persons of the past who had ventured along the various trails West: the Oregon Trail, the Santa

Fe Trail, as well as the most dangerous of all, the Smoky Hill Trail, that followed the sun east to west twelve miles to the south of my childhood home. The journals revealed a variety of insights into life one hundred and fifty years ago. The accounts became a part of the imagery of the background I referred to as I wrote my book.

I recall reading about a man and a woman traveling West with a wagon train. Somewhere in the mountains, on the way to Oregon, the woman died. She was very beautiful, and her companion — no doubt her husband — was so overcome by grief at her death that he was unable to make himself dig a customary resting place between the wagon ruts of the trail, knowing that the grave would be obliterated by the dust of the hundreds of other wagons as they passed over her. Instead, he lashed her to his back and carried her into the mountains that towered all around; he laid her to rest in an ice cave where the snow never melted and where he could find her again in his travels. His sad experience helped me to solve Pierre's dilemma when his wife Madeline died in the frozen Rockies.

Even motion pictures such as Walt Disney's *White Fang* added a dimension to my understanding of pioneer life, in its fierce portrayal of a dog fight. And *Sod House Frontier*, by Everett Newson Dick, informed me that the Plains Indians loved to eat sugar. Unfortunately, settlers terrified of the Indians sometimes laced the sugar with strychnine; the ingestion of the contaminated treat left no Indian alive to warn others of the dangers lurking in a white man's cabin.

Also, in the 1960s, the Vietnam War became a part of American life on a daily basis, and friends who had children destined to fight in that terrible war offered points of reference when I was establishing the relationships of my imaginary young people and how they faced that conflict.

Sock, a part of the *Riddle* story, was my husband's horse when he was in high school. Sock was wild and unpredictable, and one day would have killed himself and my husband by running the two of them into a moving train if my husband had not grabbed him by the bit, at the full gallop, turning him into a vertical bank next to the roadside.

Old Major, the lovable and loyal dog, lived in Kingman, Kansas, along the banks of the Ninnescah River, around 1905. He is as dear to me as if I had known him. Except for him, I would never have been born. The episode where he saved the small child was enacted in real life when my mother was a child — the only difference being that the fierce and angry cow was a roan with horns, whose calf had been taken away from her. I found an account of Old Major's heroics in my mother's memoirs, after her death.

As I was writing *Riddle of the Lost Gold*, I experienced two odd coincidences. I was unable to locate a description of the stage stops along the Smoky Hill Trail. I had obtained a list naming them, but no commentary on what they looked like. One day I chanced to visit the Butterfield Museum in Russell Springs, Kansas, southwest of Hays. While I was viewing the artifacts in the cases, my husband handed me a book entitled *Up the Smoky Hill Trail in 1867 with an Ox Drawn Wagon Train* in which the authors, Leslie and Bertha Linville, described in detail every major stage station all the way from Fort Hays to Denver. Russell Springs is a long way from anywhere. Visiting that particular museum and locating that special book was a major stroke of luck.

Yet, the strangest coincidence of all occurred when I visited the historical museum in Fort Wallace, Kansas, west of Hays. In one of the display cases, and easily read, were several pages from the journal of a cavalry soldier who had been stationed at Fort Wallace in 1867. Finding the pages was remarkable, but the fact that the dates and the accounts given were for the exact days that my own Pierre and Yvette were guests of Fort Wallace seemed beyond coincidence. A bull train — a caravan of ox-drawn wagons — really had passed through the Fort on its way to Denver! And railroad workers really were escorted by Cavalry troopers to Colorado's Raton Pass!

I have always loved a mystery. Of all the gold from Colorado that no doubt made its way east along the Smoky Hill Trail, I thought why not bury some of it at Fort Hays, to be discovered a hundred years later by two young Kansans. That scenario didn't seem at all far-fetched to me. It inspired my imagination, the characters Julia and Chris, and the *Riddle of the Lost Gold*.

Joan K. McAfee

Acknowledgments

MY APPRECIATION IS extended to Lois J. Friesen, for imparting her expertise in Creative Writing at Butler County Community College in El Dorado, Kansas, and for her critique of *Riddle of the Lost Gold*. I also want to thank Ron Parks, Curator of the Kaw Mission at Council Grove, Kansas, for suggestions after reading my manuscript.

Dr. Raymond Nelson, of Wichita, now retired from Friends University, read the work and offered valuable suggestions.

Bob Wilhelm, Superintendent of Historic Fort Hays, answered and resolved many of my questions.

The Blockhouse 1867

Chapter One

Unclaimed for a Hundred Years

*S**Late Afternoon, July 4, 1967, Western Kansas*
SHOULD I TELL him everything? Julia wondered . . . *Maybe Chris can't keep a secret!*

Julia Simmons curbed her impatience as she reined in her eager horse. She glanced eastward over her shoulder, searching the long road behind her for some sign of Chris. He had promised he would come to their special place — the limestone outcrop on a hill just two miles west of Fort Hays. Julia had arranged the meeting because she had serious matters to discuss with her friend.

But he was nowhere in sight. Julia leaned forward in her saddle.

"Come on, Honey," she urged. "Steady, now!"

Holding the reins loosely, Julia heeled her horse, laying the leather first on one side of Honey's neck and then the other. All the while Honey was zigzagging up the rocky face of the hill.

Tied behind the cantle of Julia's saddle was a small packet. It contained three articles — a letter from her brother Matt, and a handwritten book and letter from Julia's Aunt Sarah. Sarah had bequeathed to Julia the pioneer diary of their long-dead relative, Yvette Marie Prideaux. And within the diary's neatly inscribed pages was a clever riddle that when deciphered would reveal the location of a large cache of gold. Yvette's father, Pierre Prideaux, had buried the gold somewhere within the garrison of Fort Hays, once an active military post, set in the open and endless Kansas prairie to keep peace on the Plains in the midst of our nation's westward expansion. Julia's summer job at the Fort had provided her with an unexpected opportunity to search for the treasure that had eluded her family for a hundred years.

But Julia's thoughts encompassed more than Pierre's gold. She had decided to share with Chris a disquieting letter from her nineteen-year-old brother Matt, who was stationed with the U.S. Special Forces in Vietnam. While they were growing up, the younger Julia had been excluded from Matt's rough-and-tumble boyhood world. But Julia loved Matt, and when he had been sent to fight the controversial war, he left a void in her life. She had placed a picture of him, in uniform, on her dresser. His black hair and dark eyes resembled the Indians native to the Plains, though his delicate facial lines belied that heritage.

Honey quickly secured a firm foothold in the loose gravel and clumps of dirt and grass. She had a free rein to climb the hill while Julia scanned the slope, wary of the cunning prairie rattlers. Honey could sense danger quickly, and would balk in warning. But last week it had been Julia who had first heard the menacing rattle, like the sound of the wind stirring rows of hard, dry corn husks. Julia had pulled Honey back before the coiled rattler could strike.

Chapter One — Unclaimed for a Hundred Years

Today, however, there were no snakes. Upon reaching the summit, Julia dismounted. Honey's reins dangled, and she began to graze on the sparse buffalo grass that managed to thrive and send its runners over the thin gray soil.

The day was warm, but not unbearably hot. Julia settled herself on a rocky ledge and placed the letters and the book beside her. Chris was sure to arrive any minute. She sat with the sun on her back and watched the Pleasant Hill Road. In just three hours, dusk would bring on the night. To the east, a distance away, Fort Hays was barely distinguishable in the early evening glow.

Julia and Chris were summer tourist counselors at the Fort. They had just completed their junior year of high school, and because they both were knowledgeable about frontier history, they had found badly needed jobs, escorting visitors around the garrison. But Julia had never mentioned the story of Pierre's gold, for her family had kept its existence a secret. They were determined that outsiders would never gain from the hardships endured by Pierre and Yvette.

Twelve miles to the south of her vantage point, between verdant, low-lying hills, the Smoky Hill River meandered eastward. Its banks were veiled by a delicate blue haze, reminiscent of the smoke from Indian campfires long past.

Along the north side of the Smoky was the no longer used Smoky Hill Trail. Julia had heard stories, some of them tragic, about the stagecoaches, gold prospectors, and wagon trains that had followed the trail in the mid-1800s. Pierre had followed the Smoky Hill Trail, as had the Indian-fighting U.S. Seventh Cavalry and its controversial and flamboyant Lieutenant Colonel George Armstrong Custer.

The city of Hays was north and east of the Fort, on the opposite side of Big Creek. From her hilltop perch, Julia could see the huge grain elevators that dominated the horizon. Hays was an up-to-date urban community, that long ago had outgrown its pioneer beginnings.

Honey's bridle jangled faintly as she munched the grass, and Julia stirred restlessly. There was still no sign of Chris. Today he would be late. Julia shifted her position on the ledge to make herself comfortable and resigned herself to the inevitable wait.

In the pasture below the bluff, the buffalo grass was turning a soft blue-green from the recent rain. So far, western Kansas had been spared the oppressive heat that was typical of July and August.

Julia's favorite wildflowers, the white and rose Carolina anemones and delicate prairie violets, had already bloomed and died. Purple poppymallow, wavyleaf thistle, and yellow Western salsify were now tucked into corners of rough sod, grass, and rocks.

As she waited, shadows lengthened at the base of the hand-hewn limestone fence posts that were joined with rusting barbed wire. Yellow-breasted meadowlarks, with black bibs beneath their throats, perched at intervals along the twisted strands, their melodious trill a signature of the prairie.

Before long, Julia grew tired of sitting, so she stood and lifted up her arms, as if embracing the endless blue sky. She loved Kansas; she never yearned for a life different than the one into which she had been born.

Finally, Julia spotted Batese, Chris's bay, kicking up dust along the Pleasant Hill Road.

Chris — Christopher Royce Henson — would be eighteen in September, as would Julia. He was a slight five-feet-six, almost an inch shorter than Julia. He possessed an appealing outgoing personality, and that asset, along with his blond, blue-eyed good looks, easily earned him the friendship of almost everyone he met. He was a good student and a gifted athlete, and Julia thought he was the best horseman around, except perhaps for her brother Matt.

Julia recalled that it was late summer, when she was twelve years old, that she first had met Chris. The Hensons were Kansas farmers, but they were newcomers to Julia's rural community, having recently moved there from Dodge City. His family had been

Chapter One — Unclaimed for a Hundred Years

invited to the annual potluck supper held in the old country schoolhouse on the Pleasant Hill Road. From that day on, in spite of his seeming indifference to her, Chris occupied a special place in Julia's life.

Julia, her parents, and Matt lived on a farm along the Smoky Hill River. When she had learned that Chris's family had bought the nearby Kingsley place, she hoped that Chris would become her friend. But Chris wasn't interested in Julia, and found a companion in fun-loving Matt. The two boys had much in common and before long were like brothers.

By the time she was old enough to date, Julia had developed considerable natural beauty. Occasionally she assessed herself in the mirror, noticing a somewhat tall, slim figure and a golden tanned face with brown eyes, framed by dark curly hair. Yet, although she considered herself to be pretty enough, she knew Chris took no notice of her charms. Then eleven months ago, after Matt had gone to Vietnam, Chris's indifference changed to friendship, and it made the fact that Matt was not around easier for Julia to bear.

Julia heard the pounding of Batese's hooves on the road as he neared the base of the hill. Seeing Batese reminded her of the last time Matt and Chris were together, almost a year ago. It had been on a Saturday, and Chris had ridden Batese across the pasture to the Simmons' farm. Both had tried to pretend it was an ordinary day.

Like so many young men from the farm, Matt was healthy and ripe for the Draft. A college deferment was out of the question, since money was scarce at home. The rainy summer, uncharacteristic of Kansas, had been bad for dry-land farming, and to help his family survive financially, Matt was picking up and delivering freight for a local trucking company.

But the Vietnam War — thousands of miles away in a little country that seemed to have been at war with someone for years

— was escalating and the conflict was not even close to a resolution. For the first time, the local Draft Board, in Ellis County where Matt lived, was unable to fill its quota from the ranks of twenty-year-olds, and so young Matt and other boys like him were called to duty. His scheduled induction into the military was something no one in the family mentioned, as if ignoring it could stop it from happening.

That Saturday, as always, Matt rode Ginger, the horse he had raised and trained from the time she was a foal. Ginger was a brown Quarter Horse, known in the area for her ability to run the quarter mile in record time. Matt loved her as only a trainer can love his horse.

Julia had decided to ride with Matt and Chris that day. Matt would be leaving for basic training, and she wanted to spend time with him. Julia realized that when Matt was gone, a lot would change. Chris wouldn't spend his Saturdays at the Simmons' farm.

"I'll put a saddle on Colonel and go with you," Julia insisted to Matt and Chris, and she went to the barn to get her gentle Paint. She returned riding bareback, on a horse named Sock.

Sock was a three-year-old of questionable ancestry. His black head was oddly shaped, with a single, wide white stripe down his Roman nose. By reputation he was mean, bull-headed, and not-to-be-trusted. Until now, a wariness resulting from her experience with horses had kept Julia from riding him.

"Do you think you can handle that ornery cuss?" yelled Matt.

In answer, Julia kicked Sock. He responded well as he leaped into a run.

It wasn't until Julia felt herself separated from Sock's sweaty back that she fully realized the horse had no intention of acknowledging a master. He stopped abruptly and sent Julia flying. She landed on her left shoulder and slid painfully through the rough pasture grass, overgrown with thistles. Her left cheek was badly scraped and the wind knocked out of her. From the corner of her eye, she saw Sock. With his head tilted to the left to avoid stepping on the reins, he disappeared over a rise in the ground.

Chapter One — Unclaimed for a Hundred Years

Julia tried to pull her knees under her, but she couldn't move. She lay in the grass overwhelmed by pain and a good deal of humiliation. Matt quickly was beside her.

"If it were up to me, I'd shoot that damned horse!"

Julia heard Sock snort.

Batese was there with Chris, who had caught Sock and held him by the reins as he slid off Batese. Taking Sock by the bridle, Chris walked to where Julia lay, concerned for her as well.

Moments passed while Julia's lungs struggled to relax and expand enough for her to speak. In spite of Matt's protests, she slowly rose to her feet. She touched her throbbing head and felt her unruly hair, full of nettles. While Chris still held Sock by the reins, Julia grabbed a handful of his mane. With her knees wobbling, Chris boosted her onto Sock's back. For the remainder of the ride, Julia did not forget, even momentarily, what horse she was riding. When she felt Sock's muscles gather for another sudden stop, she clamped her legs tightly around his belly. Sock was unable to throw her again.

As usual, the following week, even though Matt was gone, Chris rode Batese to the Simmons' farm. Julia didn't notice the subtle change in Chris's casual greeting, as a closer friendship began to develop between the two.

The Saturday rides continued, and Julia concluded that her relationship with Chris could be compared to an incident last winter when a red-shafted flicker stunned himself by flying into her picture window. Julia had rescued the limp bird from the snowbank next to the house then held it gently, warming the soft, beautiful creature in her hands. In a short time the bird fluttered to life and struggled to free itself. Julia opened her hands, and as she watched the bird fly away, she realized the unpredictability of life. She couldn't control circumstance or events, and so she promised herself never to worry about the future or cling to something that was not there.

Now, in the soft pre-dusk light, below the bluff Batese was climbing the hill at an angle, scrambling for footing in the loose gravel. Chris shifted his weight to maintain his balance, and at the same time he scrutinized the ground, mindful of the prairie rattlers. He glanced up at Julia who was watching his ascent.

Reaching the crest of the hill, Chris dismounted and pulled off Batese's saddle and blanket. He placed them on the rock ledge and then unsaddled Honey. In companionable silence, Julia and Chris arranged the saddles and blankets into pallets. When they were finished, Chris smiled at Julia and reached into a saddlebag.

"I stopped by my camper on the way here and made us some peanut butter and jelly sandwiches." He offered one, holding out a brown paper sack.

While they ate, Chris gazed at the blue-gray hills along the river. "It's beautiful from up here, isn't it? I never get tired of it. Kansas has a sweet wildflower scent." Julia sniffed the air, inhaling the fragrance of the prairie. She sensed such profound contentment that words were inadequate to describe how she felt.

After they had finished their picnic, Julia turned to Chris. Her eyes held a hint of concern, though Chris hadn't noticed, as he settled back, making himself comfortable on his pallet.

"Got a letter from Matt today," she said.

Julia picked up her brother's letter. "It's dated June 21st, two weeks ago."

"*Dear Sis*," Julia read aloud. "*I know I didn't pay much attention to you while we were growing up, but I've always loved you. It's important to me that you know how I feel because I can't second-guess the future, especially here in this bloody place.*

"*My letters aren't censored, so I'm free to tell you what it's like to be fighting this war. I have to tell someone. Maybe then I won't feel so far away from home.*

"*The Vietnam War is 'one for the books,' Julia. And I think about Chris every day — he could get caught up in this mess, too.*"

Chapter One — Unclaimed for a Hundred Years

Julia glanced at Chris, but his face was inscrutable.
Julia resumed reading.

"*If we win this impossible war, it'll be a miracle! I'm scared most of the time, but I don't dare let it show. We're in the position of mounting an offensive against what essentially is a shadow. The Viet Cong — 'Charlie' — are experts at guerrilla warfare. They learned it when they were occupied by the French. So far, we've had no luck at all locating the Viet Cong's base. We can beat them in open combat, but then they just disappear! Gone! Where in blazes do they go? No one knows, but Charlie can appear in force whenever he chooses.*

"*That's not all. Charlie has four- and five-year-old children carrying messages and supplies. Eight-year-olds carry guns. He's even armed women who have babies on their backs! They're 'the enemy!' And the soldier who can't face that fact endangers everyone around him. I've had to put aside much of what I consider decent and learn how to fight under these circumstances.*

"*I'm often on patrol — packed light. I carry only essential equipment and live off the land — no resupply aircraft.*

"*My platoon is the best in the battalion at setting an ambush. After Charlie caught us off guard several times, we learned how to set a trap better than he does.*

"*But I want to tell you about a weird dream I had. On one reconnaissance, waiting for the Viet Cong to show up, I catnapped and while I slept, I dreamed I was in Kansas . . . with Lieutenant Kidder, part of the 1867 small detachment from Fort Sedgwick in Colorado Territory, carrying orders from General Sherman to Custer and his patrol.*

"*The men below me were riding along the headwaters of Beaver Creek, there on the state's western border. I was wearing a campaign hat and a wool and cotton uniform, like they did back then. I didn't seem to feel the heat, even though it was July and so hot the sun had curled the leaves on the buckbrush! As usual, even in my dream, only the cottonwoods didn't look parched!*

"*I was carrying a Springfield single-shot, and the other eleven men had 1863 Sharps carbines. Some of the men also had Colt*

.44-caliber revolvers. It's amazing how I could visualize all that detail . . .

"It seemed like we were in a clump of sandbar willows, about a mile from the creek, and we apparently were wending our way to the water's edge to fill our canteens. I remember looking up and seeing Pawnee Killer, the old Chief. He wasn't wearing his usual felt hat, but I recognized him and his Sioux warriors. They were crawling toward us through the bluestem and grama grass in the river bottom. I somehow knew in the dream that Pawnee Killer's backups were Cheyenne Dog Soldiers, the ones led by Tobacco and Big Head. They were on horseback, encircling us, drawing us into a net.

"It was a terrible dream . . . I knew we were dead men. I saw myself fire my one shot and watched a Sioux drop. Then suddenly, I was looking at an arrow sticking out of my left leg. I managed to load my gun and was ready to fire again . . . when I woke up.

"You know, Julia, it came to me that the Indian Wars, for Custer and his men, weren't really too different from the war I'm fighting here in Vietnam. We kill the Viet Cong like Custer and his men killed the Cheyenne at Washita River, down in Indian Territory. The Viet Cong try to annihilate our patrols a few at a time, just like Bull Bear and his Dog Soldiers did in the Cheyenne raids along the Smoky Hill Trail.

"A war is a war. It just happens that the one I'm fighting is thousands of miles from home, and my M-16 is a more sophisticated weapon than a single-shot carbine.

"I can't tell if anyone's winning. I doubt if the gurus in Saigon and Washington know either. It's frustrating not to have a clear purpose for being here. It isn't going to matter how much firepower we throw at the Viet Cong. They regroup in Laos, Cambodia, or someplace else and keep on coming. General Westmoreland should shut down the Ho Chi Minh Trail. Why doesn't he do it? Who's stopping him? We even have restrictions on where we can go into combat and what sort of damage we can inflict!

"I can't imagine where this war is headed! I just try to get by one day at a time. . .

Chapter One — Unclaimed for a Hundred Years

"These days Charlie's weaponry is upgraded. He has Soviet-built rockets and copies of Soviet weapons made in Communist China. He carries an AK-47, a lot like my M-16. He has plenty of armament to carry on a war.

"Last week, after we were pinned down by enemy crossfire, my buddy didn't make it. He'd lost too much blood. I tried to get him to the medi-vac copter they brought in, but it was no use.

"This is such a crazy war, Julia."

". . . By the way, I heard from Mom that you've inherited Yvette's journal! I hereby give you the assignment of finding Pierre's gold while I'm busy upholding the U.S. commitment to South Vietnam. It's about time someone finds his cache. A hundred years is long enough for anything to remain hidden!

"I know Yvette's riddle by heart. Maybe you can figure it out.

> Upon the Fourth a fortnight past,
> The fortress sleeps.
> The hands at five, due west.
> As heaven's light appears at dawn,
> Creeps downward, brings to notice
> Earth that welcomes gold returned to home.

"If you find the gold, you can buy me a horse ranch. Shucks! Now I definitely have to make it home! My little sister will have a fortune waiting for me!

"Your loving brother, Matt.

"P.S. Tell Mom and Dad I love them, but please don't tell all I've told you!"

Julia lowered the pages of Matt's letter until they rested in her lap. "I won't allow myself to think he might not come home!" She covered her face with her hands to hide her tears.

Chris took the letter, then slowly tore the paper into tiny pieces and tossed the scraps over the bluff. The particles caught in the air and drifted down the face of the rock, clinging and turning, until only a few white flecks were visible.

"My mother says it takes faith to get through the difficulties in life," said Chris in an effort to comfort Julia.

As Julia's tears subsided, she and Chris sat quietly in the dimming light, each alone in thought.

"I'll think about facing the Vietnam War later on. Matt has the right attitude. He'll come home, Julia. He's given himself something to live for — he wants a horse ranch!"

Julia took a long breath, knowing she was about to break the family trust.

"The only way he'll have enough money to buy a ranch is if someone in our family finds Pierre's gold. I'm determined to find it . . . I need your help, Chris. Can you keep a secret?"

"Sure, I can! I'm good at secrets." Chris had never heard of Pierre or his gold.

"Who was Pierre . . . and what happened to his gold?"

Julia picked up Yvette's journal and the letter from her aunt.

"According to Aunt Sarah," said Julia, now looking at Sarah's letter, "in 1858 my great-great-grandfather, a Frenchman named Pierre Prideaux, was living on a farm near the junction of the Marais des Cygnes and the Little Osage rivers in New Bordeaux, Missouri, near the western edge of the state. Someone handed Pierre a pamphlet explaining opportunities in the gold fields. Sarah says one article was titled *El Dorado a Reality! Gold in Kansas Territory!* All the hype about gold caused Pierre to get gold fever. Of course, before 1861, Kansas Territory extended all the way to the Rocky Mountains and included the mining camp that eventually became Denver.

"Pierre sold everything his family owned, including his farm and his blacksmith shop. In February of 1859 he purchased a book on prospecting, a covered wagon, four yoke of oxen, and a mule. In March, with his wife Madeline and his nine-year-old daughter Yvette Marie, he left New Bordeaux and traveled north to Independence, Missouri, where he turned west, following the Santa Fe Trail. Two months later at Bent's Fort, in southeastern Colorado, Pierre guided his ox team northwest. He had been following the Arkansas River and was still headed toward the Rocky Mountains.

Chapter One — Unclaimed for a Hundred Years

His destination was a settlement of tents and log cabins on the plain near Cherry Creek and the South Platte River, near Denver City. Gold had been discovered there in Clear Creek Canyon."

"Pierre must have been something of a gambler," murmured Chris.

"A gambler and much more," said Julia. "He wasn't afraid of anything. He was loyal and good to his family. But those who were not his kin thought twice before making him angry. He was a huge, black-bearded bear of a man. No one argued with him. With his Sharps rifle and his two dogs to back him up, I'm not surprised! One of the dogs was part wolf!"

"What do you know about the rest of the family?"

"Madeline was tall and strong. She had been a schoolteacher before she married Pierre.

"Yvette was a combination of the two of them; she had long chestnut hair and was a sturdy, strong little girl with a very sensitive nature. Her name was Old French, meaning 'yew bough' — a good name for her. She could bend with the wind!"

"So, Pierre was successful when he went looking for gold?" asked Chris.

"Very successful," answered Julia. "Pierre and Madeline and young Yvette spent eight years in the Rockies. That's much longer than most men prospected. He found a fortune in gold, enough to satisfy any man's dream of wealth."

Obviously curious, Chris asked, "So where is Pierre's gold now?"

"That's the mystery," said Julia. "It's buried somewhere in the garrison of Fort Hays, but no one knows where. It's said that 'the conquest of gold has brought many men misfortune.' Well, Pierre was no exception."

Chris turned and looked at the Fort in the distance, trying to imagine how it had jealously guarded such a secret for a hundred years.

"You must be kidding!" he exclaimed.

"No one in my family jokes about Pierre's gold, Chris." Julia once again looked at Aunt Sarah's letter.

"Yvette was a twelve-year-old child when she began her journal. Her account ends somewhat abruptly in 1867 when the gold was buried. By then Yvette was probably seventeen or eighteen."

"How did the gold happen to be buried at Fort Hays?" asked Chris.

"Pierre was headed back to New Bordeaux along the Smoky Hill Trail, with a wagon load of gold. That's all I know," said Julia as she turned several pages in the journal and noted the neat, legible script.

"Yvette was with Pierre and knew where he had hidden his gold. But for some reason, she left Fort Hays and didn't return to get it. She died at seventy-six without revealing its exact location. All she left as a clue was a riddle. Down through the years, most of Mom's relatives have tried, obviously without success, to find it. So far, no one has deciphered the meaning of the riddle."

"And what makes you think you'll succeed when so many others have failed?" Chris challenged. "Maybe Yvette came back for the gold and simply didn't tell anyone!"

Julia thought about this possibility, then said with conviction, "No, she didn't return to Fort Hays. I don't know how I know this; I just know. The odds of finding Pierre's gold aren't good. But that fact isn't going to stop me from trying."

In the distance, Independence Day fireworks lit up the sky. Julia and Chris watched the bursting display, then saddled their horses and rode back to the Fort, both thinking the same thing.

Where had Pierre buried his gold?

Chapter Two

A Good Campaigner

Early Evening, July 4, 1967

AFTER THE FIREWORKS, Jennifer Blake was waiting for Julia and Chris at the Tourist Information Center. Jennifer was the plump and cheerful, no-nonsense Superintendent in charge of tourism at Fort Hays. Even though she was a friend of Julia's mother, Julia received no special favors at work. Her late afternoon break that day had been an exception, and Jennifer now regretted her generosity.

"I shouldn't have given you two time off. This evening we were short-handed. Did you see the fireworks?"

Julia dismounted her horse and handed Honey's reins to Chris, who was still astride Batese.

"Yes, from the hill west of here," answered Julia.

As Jennifer waved "good-bye" to Chris, he pulled Batese around and cantered off, followed by Honey. They turned west on the Pleasant Hill Road, heading back in the direction from which they just came. Chris was going to August Janning's farm, three-quarters of a mile away, where he was living for the summer. Residing close to the Fort saved him a thirty-two-mile round trip each day.

For the past two years, Chris had driven his father's 1959 Chevrolet pickup into August's yard on his way home from school and had helped August do his chores. The two of them understood each other, and August could not think more of Chris if he were his own son.

August was a pragmatic, hard-working man of German descent. His blue eyes and lined, weatherbeaten face reflected the hours he had spent toiling in the fields. In his late seventies, with his health not good, he refused to give up farming. Occasionally, he mentioned to his wife that they should move to town, but nothing came of his talk.

For the summer, August had agreed to let Chris park both his pickup and the family's aluminum camper beside the farm's stock tank. The camper was anchored nearby, under the huge cotton-woods growing in August's south pasture. It was a good site. A rock ridge and a hollow in the hillside protected the camper from the wind.

In addition, August had allowed Chris to stable Honey and Batese in his barn in exchange for helping Mrs. Janning, who was also in her seventies. Small and wiry, she was an industrious and healthy bundle of energy who gardened prolifically and canned everything she grew. Mrs. Janning insisted upon cooking most of Chris's meals for him, exhorting him to "Eat! Eat! Or you'll waste away to nothing!"

When Chris disappeared from Julia's sight, she got into Jennifer's car for the ride into town where she lived with Jennifer and rode to work with her each day. The discipline of getting up on time was good for Julia, for she knew she was inclined to tardiness. And being late for work at the Fort was totally unacceptable.

Chapter Two — A Good Campaigner

Her first responsibility of the day was to feed and give fresh water to Old Major, the Fort's only dog. He was always patiently waiting beside his food bowl for his morning ration.

Old Major hadn't lived at Fort Hays very long. Early in June the limping, hungry, medium-sized black dog appeared on the premises. He refused to leave, and no amount of cajoling or traps could entice him to be captured. He would disappear for several days, then reappear. Finally, everyone gave up trying to outfox him. Jennifer decided to give him a home and bought him a bag of dog food. The groundskeeper named him Old Major, for he was a good campaigner, having won all his engagements!

Each day Old Major followed the military routine of the Fort. The hourly monitor of the bugle on the loud-speaker system summoned a shadowy Cavalry corps to eat, to sleep, to drill. Whatever the call required, there to respond was Old Major. He was up and about when "Reveille" sounded at sunrise and when the morning gun was fired. He was there until "Retreat" at sundown when he saw the flags lowered and heard the evening gun. At eight-thirty, "Tattoo" signaled everyone to quarters, and shortly thereafter, at nine o'clock, it was "Taps" and lights out. With the day's activities over, Old Major retired for the night to the bed Jennifer provided for him in the maintenance tool shed.

Jennifer suggested that Old Major was undoubtedly Custer's ghost, so loyal was he to Fort Hays — leaving on his "patrols," but always coming back. Custer's ghost or not, Old Major had found a home that suited him. And Julia adored him, unaware of the role he would play in her life.

Chapter Three

The House on Officers Row

July 5, 1967

ON THE MORNING of July 5th, Julia and Chris had almost no leisure time. They were kept busy escorting visitors around the Fort. Between tours they helped the groundskeeper police the premises after the Fourth of July celebration the night before.

During their lunch break, Julia and Chris discussed the matter of Yvette's journal. Deciphering the riddle was critical to solving the mystery, they reasoned. And reading the journal seemed a logical place to begin. With this in mind, they resolved to tell Jennifer about Pierre's gold and swear her to secrecy, for there was no escaping the fact that the gold was buried on state property.

Chapter Three — The House on Officers Row

After lunch, Julia and Chris approached Jennifer in her office. They were not surprised to find that she was skeptical about the gold. However, she was agreeable when Julia asked for the use of one of the houses on Officers Row. That area, usually not open to the public, was an ideal place for them to begin investigating the vague clues in Yvette's journal.

Later that day, at four o'clock, Jennifer reached into her desk and selected the key to the first house on the row.

"Let me know if you need me," she said as she handed the key to Chris.

Julia and Chris left the Center by the rear door and turned west. Old Major was right on their heels. He was especially fond of Julia, who always kept a handful of dog treats in her pocket. Within minutes, they arrived at the first of two identical white houses. Six square columns on the foremost edge supported the porch roof. A rain barrel on one end gave testimony to the lack of modern conveniences inside.

As they strolled along the boardwalk that connected the houses, Julia pointed to a level field not far from Officers Row.

"At times I try to imagine life at Fort Hays in the mid-1800s. I can picture the Seventh Cavalry on dress parade. The parade ground and flag pole were over there. If you think about it, a hundred years doesn't seem like so long ago. Can't you just see them? . . . Battle-scarred horses, men in blue and gold Cavalry uniforms, and women in long skirts and knit shawls. Sometimes the women would struggle with their skirts as they clambered aboard an ambulance, headed for an afternoon outing on the prairie while their men hunted buffalo for sport."

Chris looked where Julia pointed, then stepped onto the veranda.

"Sure, I can see them . . . Custer, and his brother Tom, 'Medicine Bill' Comstock, the Delaware Indian scouts, Custer's wife Libby — they said she was really beautiful . . . and others, too. They lived during a time that suited them. I hope they made the most of it. Cavalry soldiers had a hard life. I wouldn't have wanted to be a soldier under Custer's command!"

Chris handed Julia the key, then stood back as she unlocked the front door. Old Major, his tongue dripping saliva in the heat, ambled onto the porch behind them and flopped down in the shade under one of the windows. Chris eased his hand into Julia's pocket and pulled out a treat. He offered it to Old Major, who thumped his tail rhythmically on the wooden porch floor.

Chris and Julia stepped over the threshold and closed the solid wooden door behind them. They were standing in a wide hallway that was bright with daylight from the rows of small glass panes set in sashes surrounding the door jamb. They faced a flight of stairs that led to a landing where the steps turned and continued upward. The parlor was to their right. The room's hot, stuffy atmosphere made it difficult for them to breathe. Clearly, the house had not been aired for a long time.

"I'll open a window in the kitchen," said Julia. "You open one in the parlor."

She walked down the hallway to the community kitchen attached to the rear of the house, for the house had two apartments.

Julia quickly returned to the parlor and found that Chris was struggling to lift the sash. While she waited for him to complete his task, she surveyed the cramped quarters.

"Frontier life sure was bleak!" she commented.

In an effort at authentic decor, the stairway had been painted mustard-brown, detailed with dark-brown black walnut posts. Deer antlers nailed to the wall with big square nails served as a coat and gun rack and a catchall for any item they would hold. Julia passed her hand over the stair railing, leaving a mark. She made a mental note to find time for a thorough dusting.

The parlor was decorated with little more than the bare essentials. The white plaster walls had no closets, pictures, or wallpaper to add visual interest. A gray wool blanket served as a rug. Along the west wall, a shelf displayed an unusually attractive pendulum clock with a rural harvest scene painted on the clock's tiny glass door. Julia opened the door and looked inside. The clock's pendulum moved in a measured beat when Julia touched it with her

Chapter Three — The House on Officers Row

finger. In the northwest corner of the room a small pump organ sat under a wreath made of human hair. A kerosene lamp, its chimney black with soot, sat in another corner on a square stand. The room's two front windows were bare and were set with wavy glass that distorted the view. Arranged between the windows were two side chairs and a small table.

Julia laid the book bag containing Yvette's journal on the table and looked at Chris. "Did the Custers' live on Officers Row, or did they spend all their time in the tent they erected along Big Creek? . . . Poor Libby! It must have been tough to be married to a career military man!"

"They lived in their tent, mostly," Chris said, as he finally lifted the window sash and let in the outside air. "Maybe she preferred the men's world."

Julia nodded.

"I suppose she did, or she would have married someone else. Libby loved Custer. She seems to have been the only one who understood him."

Chris remarked, "In his day, most people were aware of Custer. He had been a Brigadier General in the Union Army during the Civil War."

"Do you believe he had political ambitions?" asked Julia. "Something I read made me think he wanted to be President of the United States."

"If Custer did consider it, he might have lost his chance," said Chris. "He was court-martialed for chasing Libby halfway across Kansas. And he was censured for other irresponsible acts: commandeering military equipment, letting the Cheyenne escape, running his men and horses ragged, and for refusing to recover the body of a dead cavalryman. Those aren't the actions of a man interested in becoming President!"

"Then maybe the White House was Libby's ambition," speculated Julia. "Well, whatever Libby's motive for marrying Custer, her life wasn't the way she dreamed it would be. They were married only twelve years when Custer was killed at Little Bighorn."

"Some people have no time at all," said Chris. "Matt was thinking about getting married when he was drafted."

Julia was stunned. "Matt . . . married? He has a *girlfriend?* . . . Who is she?"

"Someone named Elly; but he let her go. He told her he didn't want to tie her down because he didn't know if he'd be coming home."

"He should have let her wait for him," said Julia firmly.

"I would have," said Chris.

"The Vietnam War isn't going to end anytime soon," Julia continued. "According to yesterday's newspaper, Westmoreland and the field Commanders want to invade North Vietnam. The air strikes have failed. And it wouldn't surprise me to see North Vietnam invade the South. It's a mess. Some people want us to withdraw our troops."

Chris had also read the headlines.

"But if the U.S. pulls out of Vietnam, the Vietnamese government will become Communist."

Julia could not stop the tears from flowing. She turned her back to Chris. "My brother is the only thing I think about. Why should we put everything on the line for South Vietnam? Is there a good reason why Matt has to be there? Who decides these things?" She tried to dry her eyes with her hands.

Julia's back was still turned, but she could sense Chris standing close beside her. She could smell his masculine aftershave and the odor of saddle soap, for Chris had been to the barn and had cleaned the saddles earlier in the day. It took all Julia's resistance to keep from turning around to face him.

She jumped as Chris's hand touched her shoulder.

"I don't have any answers, Julia. If I did, I'd share them with the world. Come on now, don't cry. It won't solve a thing and will only make you more miserable.

"I thought we were going to read Yvette's journal. Have you tried to decipher the riddle?"

Julia dried her eyes on the handkerchief Chris gave her and tried to will her heart back to a normal rhythm.

Chapter Three — The House on Officers Row

"Yes, but not everything adds up," she answered. She pushed the book bag to the center of the table and sat down.

"What doesn't add up?" Chris asked as he pulled out his chair.

"Well, for one thing, Yvette began the riddle by giving a date — *'Upon the Fourth,'* with a capital F. That would be Independence Day. *'A fortnight past'* would put the date at July 18th. I thumbed through the journal until I found the entry made on July 14th. The next dated entry was made on the twentieth. On the eighteenth it appears Pierre was still on the trail. There seems to be a five-day time lapse where something occurred.

"*'The fortress sleeps.'* All Yvette said was that people were asleep at the Fort on the morning of July 18th. So what? Most of Kansas was probably asleep — that is, assuming it was night. The riddle doesn't make sense."

"It makes sense if we can find the proper way to look at it," said Chris. "Anything else?"

"*'The hands at five, due west.'* A compass doesn't have numbers on it. The hand always points north. If it refers to the time of day, the clue states the Fort was asleep at five o'clock the morning of July 18th. No year was given, but it had to be 1867. Due west is a specific direction. What does *due west* have to do with anything? That part of the riddle doesn't seem relevant to me.

"*'As heaven's light appears at dawn'* is simple. The sun came up.

"The next line, *'Creeps downward, brings to notice.'* I think *creeps* is a curious word to use!

"And the last line, *Earth that welcomes gold, returned to home.*

"I conclude that the gold is buried. But I still have no idea where to look for it."

Chris couldn't improve upon Julia's deductions.

"Let's read Yvette's journal," he suggested. "Maybe something will come to mind."

Chris could sense Julia's determination as she opened the book bag and he had a feeling of high adventure at the prospect of solving the riddle and making Matt's dream come true.

"I'll read," said Julia. "Perhaps I should begin with the entries Yvette made in 1867. That's the year the gold was buried."

Soon Julia and Chris were engrossed in a time long gone.

Chapter Four

The Siren Song of Gold

December 25, 1866

𝒫INE BOUGHS GRACE our fireplace ledge, and an Advent wreath is centered upon our humble table, for today is Christmas.

With great joy I received fresh pages for my journal, a lead pencil, and a pastry. The pastry brought back fond memories, for many years ago in New Bordeaux, on Christmas Day Mother never failed to bake Pebble Dash pie for me and the other children. How my cousins and I loved the sweet treat! This year Mother once again baked the pie, using precious sugar from her larder. I became a rapt pupil as I watched her line four pie tins with pastry, then mix together one-half pint molasses, one-half pint water, one teaspoon baking soda, and one teaspoon vinegar. This mixture she divided into the prepared pie tins. She sifted one-half pound wheat flour with one-half pound oat flour. To the flour she added six ounces sugar and one-half pound lard, for she had no butter. With her hands she rubbed the flour and lard into small crumbs, then sprinkled the crumbs over the molasses to be baked over a moderate heat until the pastry crust was brown.

I have made a promise to myself. Sometime in the future I shall return to New Bordeaux, for at night I dream of the home I knew as a child. The carefree childhood that should have been mine is gone, but Missouri is still there. Someday I shall bake Pebble Dash pie for my own children. I shall not let go of my dreams.

The Rocky Mountains are majestic and I love their beauty, but at times I think Father does not plan to leave this tiresome place. He is all enthusiasm for the claim he bought from George Jackson along the south fork of Clear Creek. Its stream bed becn's to him, urging him to find more gold in its nugget-laden sandbars. Father's partner, Anton Dumler, is a driven man who also covets the gold in Clear Creek. Father does not approve of Mr. Dumler and has told Mother and me that Mr. Dumler is a foolish and greedy man. His great ambition is to live in San Francisco along the Barbary Coast. No doubt he yearns for enough gold so that he can spend his life in the gambling dens along Pacific Street.

Father and Mr. Dumler have already panned the easiest gold to obtain. It was there for the picking along the biggest sandbar. Father's share is safely hidden (from Mr. Dumler) in an abandoned gold mine, stored in leather pouches. Father cannot trust Mr. Dumler. He lacks discipline, and when he is in Denver City, he sometimes loses a season's hard work in a single game of poker!

Chapter Four — The Siren Song of Gold

Before winter had set in, Mr. Dumler and Father diverted the stream. They knew they were forbidden to do this by common consent of all the miners. They ignored the law in order to take out the gold close to bedrock. At first, Father was not willing to change the flow of water. However, Mr. Dumler insisted upon it. Deviation of the water flow cheats the miners downstream from us. I fear they shall discover what we have done and take reprisal!

December 31, 1866

Mother must soon consult a dentist. She still has a toothache. Yesterday I split a raisin, sprinkled it with cayenne pepper and put it on her gum. She said it was a great help, but I know she is suffering.

I think the weather is moderating. Ice fell from our roof today.

January 12, 1867

I have neglected my journal for some days. Our rude log house, which has only a door and one window, is dimly lit. The window is covered with deerskin to keep out the wind. Inside we have difficulty seeing well enough to read or do embroidery, having only the light from our fireplace for illumination. We are frugal with our tallow candles.

We still have sufficient firewood. Last fall Father and Mr. Dumler took leave from their work for several extra hours each day to cut trees for our winter's supply of wood. This was fortuitous. Along with the cold and the wind, we have had heavy accumulations of ice and snow. We are grateful for the warmth of a fire, even though its comfort seldom reaches the far corners of our cabin.

January 15, 1867

Today Mother folded back the piece of deerskin covering our tiny window. A welcome ray of light brightened the interior of our dwelling. We make use of the deerskin, for it helps to stay the wind from ruining the oiled parchment we use for a glass windowpane.

I have laid aside the handiwork that has filled endless winter hours and resumed my lessons. Many years ago, Mother decided to become my teacher. With Mother tutoring me, it is not difficult for me to progress in my studies. In New Bordeaux I hated my lessons! Miss Symes, the schoolmistress, was cruel-hearted. I was not the only one she abused. The other children, one by one, were her victims when they did not cipher correctly or do their script to suit her.

My best friend Hannah often could not master her sums. To punish her for her inability to be accurate, one day Miss Symes fed the slices of buttered bread in Hannah's tin lard bucket to Jonas Riedel's dog who, in all weather, waited for Jonas beside the schoolhouse door. That day at noon I gave Hannah my apple.

Under such stressful circumstances I failed with many of my assignments. However, with Mother's instruction my penmanship is neat and legible. I speak, read, and write both English and French. I am now able to cipher accurately, although I am not fond of numbers. Father has told me it does not matter that I am a girl. He is proud of my accomplishments!

When I was a child, sometimes I wondered if Father

Chapter Four — The Siren Song of Gold

wished for a son instead of a daughter. Now I am certain he loves me as I am.

January 20, 1867

Oh, dreary, endless days! We have listened to Clear Creek's staccato splashing on the rocks in its stream bed for almost eight years. We have been closed in by the winters, and all of us wait impatiently for the spring thaws. We think only of the gold.

Cursed gold! I am caught in its trap. Like it or not, as a dutiful daughter, Father's quest for gold has also become mine. Each year with the first thaw I put aside my lessons. I am in my father's care for the entire day. We pan the gravel and fine black sand in the stream bed looking for "colors," tiny flecks of gold trapped in the cheater riffles of the pan.

My long skirts, which I prefer to trousers, become heavy with wet sand. A sunbonnet shades my face, and I wear long sleeves to protect my arms. Unfortunately my hands are exposed to the elements and quickly become sore and burned by the sun. My knees and back ache from endless hours spent squatting over the mountain stream.

All day I scrape the gravel and black sand into my pan and immerse the whole into Clear Creek's running water. I am always turning and shaking the pan and throwing out the bigger chunks of rock, letting the stream carry away the worthless sediment. Occasionally, I hit the pan very hard to settle the gold. At first, because I was not skillful I washed it away. However, with time and patience I learned how to rock the pan from side to side, thus helping the larger pieces of gold to remain in the sand along with numerous tiny gold flakes.

The black sand is called magnetite. I collect it in a jar. At night I dry it and pick out the gold. I have become skillful in my efforts to find and capture the yellow temptress!

January 25, 1867

Another winter storm tears at our dwelling. I am ashamed to complain about my discomfort. Father and Mother have worked diligently to provide a suitable home for us. This wretched hovel does not keep out the cold, especially when the wind blows unceasingly!

February 1, 1867

Our dwindling supply of firewood is a matter of concern. Mr. Dumler, who lives on the opposite side of Clear Creek, is less in peril. He has built a comfortable dwelling about ten yards up the side of the mountain. He calls his house a "dugout." It is somewhat like a cave, with a wooden door at the entrance.

My parents discussed the merits of a dugout. There were many, but Mother recalled the black depths of the abandoned mine that hides our gold. She decided that she did not want to live in a cave.

February 5, 1867

I yearn for spring to bring us relief from our confinement! We cannot live in Denver City during the winter as some miners do. Moral depravity is rampant and drunkenness is

Chapter Four — The Siren Song of Gold

common, although we have been told some good men are trying to improve the city.

I pray for an end to the business of harvesting the gold in Clear Creek. Father and Anton Dumler have torn the sandbar apart down to the solid rock, looking for the gold nuggets that seem to be found in every pan of drag.

I recollect my first glimpse of gold. I had turned the nugget over and over in the palm of my hand. It did not glitter. Its color looked the same from any angle. It had lain in the water for a long time, but it was not tarnished or rusted. Father struck a small piece with a hammer to demonstrate to me that pure gold does not shatter but instead is malleable.

Father gleans every fleck of gold from the drag. Tiny pieces cling to quicksilver, and Father separates them by first putting them together in a wet chamois bag. Then he squeezes the bag and the quicksilver passes through the pores of the wet leather. The gold never does.

One day I asked Father what had formed the gold. He said that in past ages the molten rock deep inside the earth heaved upward into mountains. As the liquid rock cooled over the centuries, veins of pure gold were enclosed in quartz or other worthless gangue. Somewhere upstream, he told me, a mother lode was exposed to the elements. Over time, various sized chunks of gold were dislodged and were carried downstream where they came to rest in the quiet waters of our sandbars. Occasionally, Father and Mr. Dumler look for the mother lode. So far, their search has been unsuccessful.

February 12, 1867

Father still does not know why George Jackson was willing to sell his claim to the gold in Clear Creek. Mr. Jackson knew he would be rich if he stayed and worked the site. He was young and healthy, yet one day he named a price. Father bought Mr. Jackson's claim for far less than it was worth.

After he collected his money, Mr. Jackson left Denver City. Mr. Jackson's partner was Anton Dumler. Therefore, he became my father's partner. They marked their claim with the location, their names, and the filing date, then listed it with the district recorder.

Perhaps it is indiscreet of me to comment, but I cannot abide Mr. Dumler. The times when Mother finds it her Christian duty to include him in our family circle are the hardest for me to endure. If I am not alert, he sits beside me and attempts to entertain me with tales of his native Pennsylvania. Usually, I find it convenient to stand near the fire when he is in our cabin.

February 17, 1867

Although Father has cut more trees for firewood, our food supplies are scant. He now fears our staples shall be depleted before the spring thaw. We are almost out of flour, bacon, and coffee.

The winters are always a trial for Father and Mr. Dumler. They wait impatiently for spring, hoping the time shall pass quickly, as do Mother and I.

March 2, 1867

The hot mineral springs close by our cabin, where we bathe even in winter, are a source of joy to all of us and make our lot in life less difficult. The circumstance of living

Chapter Four — The Siren Song of Gold

in the wilderness has caused our family unaccustomed hardships. Mother yearns for the vegetable and herb gardens she lovingly tended in New Bordeaux, for at times we have had little food on the table. We had never experienced deprivation until we came to live in Clear Creek Canyon.

But yesterday, good fortune smiled upon us. Father shot a deer that was grazing in the high meadow below the timberline. Now we have fresh venison.

Our dogs, Bruno and Pride, were ravenous. We must keep them well fed, for we have need of them. Claim jumpers hurriedly move on upon seeing the dogs' fangs and Father's Sharps rifle.

Pride belongs to Father; Bruno is my dog. A more gentle and loving creature than Bruno has never graced God's earth. At least it seems so to me. How we acquired the two dogs is a dreadful tale; the story can only be partly chronicled. Mr. Dumler's account of the incident left much unstated. I shudder when I think of what happened.

Two summers ago Mr. Dumler had business in Denver City, a small settlement thirty miles east of our claim, near the entrance to Clear Creek Canyon. On the afternoon of the day he was to return to our claim, he witnessed a dog fight in the street. In the center of a circle of rowdy men who were laying bets on the outcome of the fight were an Eskimo dog and a large black cur. The two dogs were engaged in mortal combat. At the conclusion of the fight, the cur lay dead, his neck broken. Left unharmed was the Eskimo dog, his jowls dripping blood. Immediately after this execution of savagery, the Eskimo dog became as tame as a lap dog. He wanted only a pat from his master's hand as a reward for his bravery.

Mr. Dumler had placed a bet on the outcome of the fight. True to his usual luck, Mr. Dumler lost the bet, for his gold was on the cur. Other men also lost their gold and soon an altercation took place. Someone accused the Eskimo dog's owner of cheating; they suggested that he had poisoned the cur prior to the fight.

The truth shall never be known, for someone in the crowd had a gun. Shortly, the dog's owner lay dead; the gold he had collected was scattered upon the ground.

Men scrambled to grasp the dead man's gold, including Mr. Dumler. However, it soon became apparent that the gold would be collected at a price. Two dogs guarded the man's body, one the Eskimo dog who had won the battle in the street. The other was a fierce wolf-like animal with glittering, icy-blue eyes.

The angry combatants wanted to shoot the dogs, but a more compassionate man interceded. "Let them live," he said. "It's enough that a man has died."

"When it became apparent to Mr. Dumler that soon the other men would leave, he waited. By late afternoon the last had departed.

Mr. Dumler told us that he was alone in the street and facing the two dogs who would not let him near the man's body. Mr. Dumler was certain that the man's pockets contained gold, and he plotted ways to lure the dogs away from the man. At last, he formulated a plan. He reached into his parcel of belongings and removed a large quantity of jerky. Then piece by piece, he threw the chunks of dried meat at the dogs; each time the meat fell farther away from the man's body. At last he was able to grasp the man by his boots and pull him forward, whereupon he lifted the man across his shoulders and quit the town.

Along the trail back to our claim, he stopped and searched the man, finding little gold. Before continuing on his way, it is to Mr. Dumler's credit that he placed the body of the man in a rock crevice and pushed heavy boulders across the opening, preventing wild animals from ravaging the grave.

Mr. Dumler soon realized that the two dogs were following him, for his clothes carried their owner's scent. As Mr. Dumler did not want the dogs, Father took them in. Father has always had a way with such creatures, and soon the dog who was part wolf, whom he named Pride, was eating from his hand.

Mother feared the dogs and asked Father to pen them outside, but I was not afraid of them. I sat on a footstool and scrutinized Bruno, the dog who had killed the cur. After a time a whimper escaped him, and he turned his eyes away from my gaze. When I snapped my fingers, he came to me and laid his head in my lap. It was then, with Father's consent, that I claimed him as mine.

March 5, 1867

Today Mother and I set about curing a portion of the venison. To each gallon of water we added: one and one-half pounds salt, one-half pound sugar, one-half ounce saltpetre, and one-half ounce potash. We boiled, skimmed, and cooled these ingredients. Then we placed the venison in deep crocks, pouring the cooled liquid over the meat, covering it well, to remain four or five weeks. Three days earlier, I had sprinkled the fresh meat with powdered saltpetre to remove the surface blood. The task was not to my liking, but I did my share of work without argument. Putting the venison down in pickle is the only way to assure ourselves a supply of meat.

Father has tied portions of the venison on the cold roof of our cabin, but predators are bound to catch its scent. The very day that Father secured the meat, that night a grizzly bear got wind of the blood and climbed onto the pine rafters over our heads. The enormous weight of the bear caved in the roof on one corner. Only the grace of God prevented him from plunging into the interior. The bear was able to steal a goodly share of our meat, but the bear was not alone in his endeavors. A cougar also coveted his share. When I heard the big cat scream, I was rendered unable to move. The sound was frightening, like a woman in terrible pain. Father loaded his gun and, through the window, fired it into the underwood across Clear Creak. He did not kill the cougar, for in the distance, we heard his departing scream. Pride and Bruno were in a frenzy and spent several hours frantically tearing at their pen and barking.

That night we slept in Mr. Dumler's dugout.

March 15, 1867

This morning Father informed Mother and me he was considering a trip to Doyle's General Store in Denver City. He sat at the table with Mother, filled several tiny leather pouches with gold dust, and planned what to purchase.

Mother was afraid for his safety and did not want him to make the trip. She counseled him to abandon his plan, as the idle placer miners in Denver City who have no claims would soon be aware of his gold and would think of ways to rob him. She reminded him that the snow in the canyon is deep, and at this time of year, the trip is very dangerous. She also reminded him that we are not without bullets and gunpowder and can survive until spring. Mother's final arguments were heeded by Father.

Waiting for the time when I can return to New Bordeaux is tiresome. I am lonely and I yearn to meet young people

Chapter Four — The Siren Song of Gold

my own age. This forced solitude is a burden I would bear for no one except my beloved father.

March 17, 1867

Winter is still upon us, but we have determined it is perhaps the middle of March. It is likely we have lost track of time, for the tedious hours slip by and sometimes we fail to mark the passing of a day.

However, this morning was certainly not dull, for Mother was in tears and Father and I were filled with consternation. The brooch that Father gave to Mother three Christmases past was missing from the shelf where she keeps her looking glass and other special items. It was a most exceptional piece, made of delicate gold filigree, and very old, with a fiery opal in its center. Mother did not say so, but I suspect she believes Mr. Dumler took the brooch, for he was in our cabin collecting a loaf of bread that Mother had offered him. We have no proof of this, however, and can only speculate on its disappearance.

March 19, 1867

Father has promised both Mother and me, upon his word of honor, we shall soon leave Clear Creek Canyon. His good fortune and hard labor has secured enough gold to last each one of us for a lifetime!

March 21, 1867

Home! How the word sings in my heart! The prospect

fills me with joy! Yesterday Father confided to Mother and me that we shall return to New Bordeaux as soon as the spring thaws come and travel is possible. We shall go regardless of Mr. Dumler's thoughts on the matter.

That evening there was merriment in our cabin, for although we lack instruments, Father sang love songs to Mother and kissed her when he thought I would not notice! At first, I pretended to sleep. Then I did slumber; I was so cozy and warm under my bearskin cover. Before I slept, Father sang an old French folk song in his deep melodious voice, so filled with contentment. I record it here lest my memory dims in later years as age overtakes me. The words shall forever carry me back to the Rocky Mountains, to my parents, and to my life in Clear Creek Canyon.

Au Clair de la Lune

Au clair de la lune, Mon ami Pierrot;
Prete moi ta plume, Pour ecrire un mot.
Ma chandelle est morte, Je n'ai plus de feu;
Ouvre moi ta porte, Pour l'amour de Dieu.
Au clair de la lune, Pierrot repondit:
Je n'ai pas de plume, Je suis dans mon lit.
Va chez la voisine, Je crois qu'elle y est,
Cardans sa cuisine On bat le briquet.

At Pierrot's Door

With the moon's pale shimmer, little friend Pierrot,
Shines thy candle's glimmer on the fallen snow.
Lend a pen, I pray thee, but a word to write,
One farewell to say thee ere I go tonight.

See my lantern flicker, now the light is out;
Now the snow falls thicker, round and round about.
Gusts go helter-skelter, lo the night is old!
Ope and give me shelter ere I die of cold!

Chapter Four — The Siren Song of Gold

The words are so poignant! "Little friend Pierrot . . . lo, the night is old! Ope and give me shelter, ere I die of cold!"

April 8, 1867

Perceptible shoots of green grass in rock crannies far from the meadow beside the hot springs, a warm breeze, and the call of wild geese indicate spring is coming. What a joyful prospect!

Today Father and Mr. Dumler began the journey to Doyle's General Store in Denver City. They plan to be gone at least ten days to find a dentist for Mother, replenish our supplies, and mail letters to friends and relatives at home. Hopefully, mail from New Bordeaux shall be waiting for us at the tiny postal exchange in the General Store.

Father carried only enough gold dust to buy necessities. He also took Pride and his Sharps rifle, leaving Bruno and his Springfield rifle with me. I pray we shall have no need of the gun. Mother has conquered her fear of our dogs. Tonight Bruno shall sleep inside our cabin to guard and comfort us.

April 26, 1867

Father and Mr. Dumler returned to us safely today after an absence of eighteen days. The ice and snow in the canyon made their trip hazardous.

They brought good news! A dentist, or at least someone who pulls teeth, has opened an office in Denver City. Father plans to take Mother to consult him. Mr. Dumler availed himself of the man's services, though to my dismay, he deemed the dentist less than competent.

Along with the staples, they brought back several copies of the *Rocky Mountain News*. It seems Denver City has a newspaper and is becoming quite civilized! They also brought us letters from relatives in New Bordeaux and an old copy of the *Harper's Weekly*, describing battles of the Civil War. The war ended in 1865 having been won by the North. It was an unusually bloody conflict waged between brothers. Yet, one good came of it. The practice of slavery in our country is no more.

How eagerly we perused our letters from home, delighting in every word! Our letters to them had told of our plan to return to New Bordeaux. We have all changed since our tearful parting so long ago. I pray we shall be able to pick up the fabric of our lives as if we had never gone looking for gold but had been amongst them all these past years.

Father remarked to me that except for the difficulty of breaking trail, his journey was without incident. When he thought I was asleep, however, I overheard him tell Mother he had observed Mr. Dumler in animated conversation with two men. Father knew one of them, Jacques St. John, a big man with closely set black eyes. St. John is considered by many people to be bad company. The other man was not known to Father. He was of middle height with weather-burned features. Upon inquiry, Father was told he was a merchant named Charles Atkinson. The man worked for a freight line, bringing all manner of goods to Denver City. Later, when Father confronted Mr. Dumler, he denied he had visited with anyone.

April 30, 1867

The cold weather has moderated. However, the spring rains and melting snow have caused the stream to run full.

Chapter Four — The Siren Song of Gold

The swiftly moving water is tearing at the banks of Clear Creek and ruining much of Father's and Mr. Dumler's hard labor.

No matter; they have returned to the sluice they built along the diverted stream on their claim. They shovel sand from the exposed stream bed into a long wooden trough as water flows over it, washing away the light soil and allowing heavy particles of gold to sink to the bottom where they are caught by the riffles.

What they are doing to the water flow is surely causing other miners downstream a great deal of difficulty. I know Father is uncomfortable with what they have done. I have heard him arguing about it with Mr. Dumler, who shows not the slightest concern. In any case, together they have dug a shaft downward along the exposed stream bed looking for rich gold samples as they work. Last fall, before the snow and ice made us prisoners in our homes, the sand and sediment in their trench yielded them a rich pay streak, which they sifted down to bedrock.

May 1, 1867

Spring is indeed upon us! Unfortunately, the weather is foul much of the time. Mother waits impatiently for her trip to see the dentist, but travel is still not possible. The inclement weather also prevents working the sluice, causing Mr. Dumler and Father to have short tempers.

May 7, 1867

Mother's affection for Father, certainly not the gold, was what brought her to Clear Creek Canyon. In truth, she had little choice in the matter, for she depends upon Father for everything. He is the source of strength for both of us, and our regard for him has no limit.

Still, our existence is tedious. Mother and I both yearn for the company of other women. What joy it would be to converse with friends over a cup of hot tea! It has been three years since we have seen our own kind.

May 10, 1867

I pray for improvement in the weather. Mother cannot wait much longer to consult a dentist, for she is constantly in pain. We shall travel in spite of the danger if relief is not forthcoming.

Mr. Dumler had two teeth pulled at the time he and Father went for supplies. According to Mr. Dumler, the dentist claimed his extractions were painless. He attributed it to the efficacy of a device that sends an electrical current through the tooth. Mr. Dumler tried it, but he did not think the dentist's method was as good as he claimed it to be.

Mr. Dumler's opinion of the dentist does not matter. Mother must avail herself of his services. She has a brave face, but I perceive she is afraid. Because I love her, I too am filled with fear.

May 15, 1867

Tragedy has struck our lives. Mother is gravely ill. Without Father's knowledge or approval, evidently because she knew of Mr. Dumler's forceps, Mother begged Mr. Dumler to pull her bad tooth. I cannot fathom why Mother decided

Chapter Four — The Siren Song of Gold

to avail herself of Mr. Dumler's services. While Father and I worked the sluice, Mother had approached Mr. Dumler and had convinced him that he was capable of pulling her bad tooth.

Later, Father asked Mr. Dumler why he had not earlier made known that he was willing to assist in this manner. Mr. Dumler's answer was evasive. He had not mentioned it, he said, because he was not comfortable interfering in our family's business.

The deed was accomplished, but Mr. Dumler's explanation concerning his ability to pull teeth did not have the ring of truth. Until that moment, I had never seen my father when he was angry. I refuse to give all the details of how he forced Mr. Dumler to admit his lie!

In any case, Mr. Dumler confessed that he had never before pulled anyone's bad tooth. He claimed the dentist in Denver City harbours a weakness for gambling. When Mr. Dumler played poker with the dentist for a pot of Pike's Peak gold coin, the dentist put the case containing his forceps on the table when he had no more gold. Mr. Dumler held the winning hand, taking everything.

Father accepted this explanation. In my opinion, Mr. Dumler should not have kept the case of dental tools, much less made use of them.

After Father extracted Mr. Dumler's confession, he cowered inside his dugout for many hours, afraid to show his face. After a time he left the dugout, taking with him a backpack and his gun. I found him along the bank of Clear Creek. He was holding a cold wet towel over his nose, attempting to sooth his wounded face. He allowed as how Father had broken his ribs. He was headed down the canyon, he said, to find a doctor. He told me that he was sorry Mother was suffering. He also remarked that if a doctor was available in Denver City, he would surely bring him up the canyon to treat Mother. He left without confronting Father about the fate of their claim.

May 18, 1867

Mother died just before sunup, after many hours of agonized suffering. When she could no longer see the candle Father held aloft as I ministered to her needs, I knew death was near. Our love had no power against unyielding fate.

Two days earlier, with trepidation and tears, Father had sharpened his bowie knife. Using the cumbersome blade, he endeavored to cut a slit along the underside of Mother's jawbone in an effort to drain the accumulation of purulent matter. It was to no avail. Her once beautiful face, now so bruised and swollen, refused to heal.

For our family to have succumbed to the lure of gold, even to my mother's death, leaves me devastated. We had enough gold within two years of working George Jackson's claim to have lived like kings for the rest of our lives. The prospect of more and yet more gold kept us from turning our backs on Clear Creek Canyon. What we have wrought plagues us like a mad dream from which we cannot awaken.

Chapter Five

Farewell to Clear Creek Canyon

Along the Trail, Day 2

OUR DESTINATION IS Denver City. For the past two days we have kept away from trails where we might cross paths with Mr. Dumler on his way back to the claim. Father is avoiding a confrontation with him. I set down this account as the sun sinks in the west.

Mother's death brought to Father and me the problem of where she should be buried. Although spring was in evidence, the ground was frozen; it was not an option for Father to dig a grave. In spite of it, Father prepared her body for burial. Before dawn he hurried to the mining site. There he removed one side of the wooden sluice, cut it in half, then dragged one of the slabs inside the cabin and placed it on several large kegs. After covering the plank with a quilt, we laid Mother's body upon it. With loving hands we bathed her, and when she was dressed, we brushed and arranged her hair in a manner that managed to conceal her wounded face. Then Father placed Mother's missal, her rosary, and her own mother's locket in her hands and wrapped her tightly in the quilt. Next, Father used a hand auger to make holes along the sides of the plank and tightly lashed Mother's body to the board, leaving lengths of rawhide for hand grips. By stooping under the board, Father lifted it from the kegs and dragged it outside into the cold, gray morning mist.

Father's destination was the mine where he had hidden our gold. For more than an hour we struggled — he with his burden and I with our essential supplies, through the underwood along the banks of Clear Creek, downstream from our cabin. Twice, Father was forced to wade in the stream where he slipped on the wet rocks. He did not fall, and eventually he guided us to an almost perpendicular rock precipice, over thirty feet in height, the uppermost level being a shelflike protuberance. At the base of the cliff, where Clear Creek formed a bend, the rushing water constantly splashed against the large boulders in the stream bed, creating a rainbow in the spray.

When we reached the cliff, Father placed the litter in an upright position, leaning it against the rock wall.

Among the things I carried, Father had given me a bucket, several candles, matches, and a long length of cordage. Taking the cordage, he proceeded to instruct me on how to secure the litter, for he planned to elevate Mother's body up the side of the mountain to the rock ledge above us.

Chapter Five — Farewell to Clear Creek Canyon

After I had received my instructions Father turned away, disappearing into the underwood next to the cliff, leaving me alone with Mother.

I squatted in the sand to wait, and with an aching heart, I stared at the bundle that was lashed to the litter. In my mind's eye, I could see Mother's natural face as the light from our fireplace illuminated her countenance. I closed my eyes, and at once, I felt her presence. Strangely, I also heard her voice.

"Yvette, you must not worry about me. All is well."

A feeling of peace came over me, for Mother's words had quelled my fears.

When I opened my eyes I saw Father's face high above me, peering over the edge of the cliff. When the end of his rope reached me, I tied it to the litter. Then I stood back and watched as Father slowly pulled Mother's body up the face of the rock.

Mother's ascent accomplished, Father lowered the rope once again. I gathered up the bucket, the candles, and other supplies and tied the rope around them. When the rope lowered a third time, I fastened it around my waist. Aided by Father, I climbed to the narrow ledge where he was waiting for me. By now it was early afternoon.

The ledge, however, was not Father's destination. He began a second ascent up the side of the mountain. This time into a partially concealed fissure, cut deep into the north face of the canyon. Some distance into the fissure was the roughly framed opening to the mine. I watched as Father wrestled aside a dead pine tree, hanging from its roots above us. Its gnarled branches almost covered the entrance. Beyond the entrance, the dark recess concealed a small dry tunnel.

When I entered the mine, for the first time in many years I saw our gold. So *much* gold! There were many stacks of leather pouches, each one, I knew stuffed with coin, nuggets, or gold dust.

Not caring what was in the pouches, Father tossed more than a score of the gold-filled bags into the tunnel's shadowy recess where he used them to form a rude support for Mother's funeral bier. Once the bier was situated, Father gently unfolded the quilt from around Mother's face and arranged her rosary and missal. My grandmother's locket, he handed to me. God witnessed our many tears as we knelt at Mother's side and said the rosary. Eventually I stood up, but Father continued to kneel at Mother's side. He declared he could not leave her thus; his tears were like December rain as he again folded the quilt over her beloved face.

In time, although grief lay heavily upon him, Father turned his attention to the gold. Along with the other supplies, Father had brought with him several large leather pouches and some strips of rawhide. He handed one of the pouches to me. I filled it with as much gold as I could carry, ignoring my aching shoulders, as from time to time, I tested the weight of my load. Father filled his own pouches with many times the weight of my own burden.

The sun was low in the sky when we quit the mine. Only a few hours of daylight remained. Father remarked that there was scant time to finish our joyless task. Therefore, we laid our pouches aside. The two of us gathered dry timbers from the darkened depths of the shaft. With them Father built an adequate fire near the mine's entrance, for we needed warmth and a degree of protection from wild animals.

Food had not been a concern earlier in the day, and in our grief we had failed to provide ourselves sustenance. Hunger was our companion. Father insisted we must eat something if we were to finish our endeavors. He searched out a cluster of pinon pines, gathered a quantity of cones, then tossed

Chapter Five — Farewell to Clear Creek Canyon

them into the fire. The heat roasted and loosened the seeds. After Father had broken the cones apart, we found that the seeds were edible.

The hour was now late, and fatigue overcame both of us as we prepared our makeshift beds. Our gold-filled pouches would have to serve as pillows. We each fashioned a resting place with boughs and then lay down by the fire. Sleep came quickly.

The following morning in the pre-dawn light, I searched for Father. I found him quietly sleeping next to my mother. Seeing them thus was more than I could bear. The peace I had earlier found was shattered. I cried again, and when I stopped crying, no more tears would come.

I would never see the face of my beloved mother again. I waited in the cold outside the mine until Father awoke. When he appeared, we began to tightly seal the mine's entrance, using such rocks and stones that were at hand as well as mud from the stream bed. At one point, Father loaded a pouch with gold and returned to the cabin for a mallet and a chisel. When he returned, with the tools he fashioned a keystone from a large flat rock, which he wedged into the opening of the mine, locking the other rocks in place. We covered our handiwork with the rotting pine tree and endeavored to hide the evidence of our labor.

It was noon when we returned to the cabin. We had no interest in food. After feeding the dogs, we went directly to bed. Our labor had taken its toll, and we both slept as though we, too, were dead.

When we stirred from our slumbers, it was late in the day. We had not eaten a substantial meal for many hours. Father decided we should partake a supper of johnnycake, molasses, and coffee. He did not forget Pride and Bruno and fed them the last of our fresh venison.

This done, he selected clean clothing for himself and went to bathe at the springs. When he returned, Father insisted I should also bathe and don a calico dress, my cowhide boots, a man's wool coat, and a shawl. Then Father entered our cabin and carried outside Mother's teakwood chest. It contained her letters from home and the embroidered linens she had carefully packed away; she had been saving the beautifully worked pieces for the day when she would return to New Bordeaux. He also brought outside her looking glass. That memento he gave to me. He threw into the fireplace Mother's dresses and mine, as well as my sunbonnet and his own personal possessions. Father handed me my tortoiseshell comb, a crucifix, my journal, and my prayer book.

Our household goods he left in the cabin, first laying aside two fur pelts, a leather water pouch, and a tin grub box with a hinged lid. The grub box contained coffee, a coffee pot, and a horn-handle hunting knife. He added tin plates, cups, forks, a frying pan, and a small hollow wooden cylinder containing lucifer matches. Those items, along with measured portions of cornmeal, sugar, flour, baking soda, salt, lard, bacon, raisins (Father's Christmas gift to my mother), crackers, and dried venison comprised staples for a trip. With guns and ammunition, our provisions were complete.

Our necessary supplies, in addition to the gold, made the assemblage very heavy. At the last minute, Father reluctantly put sizeable packs on Pride and Bruno, who didn't seem to mind being pressed into service. To my surprise, he also lashed Mother's teakwood chest to the pouches he had packed with gold. Then he secured almost everything else on the back of our old mule who had spent his life grazing in the green grass that flourishes around the hot springs.

The sun was behind the trees when everything was

Chapter Five — Farewell to Clear Creek Canyon

in readiness. Father informed me that at last, we were returning to New Bordeaux.

Once again Father and I slept, and the next morning after checking the loads our animals carried, we shouldered our heavy gold-filled pouches. As I took one last look at the interior of our cabin, the place where so much of my life had been lived, I reflected upon my many years along Clear Creek with Mother as my sole female companion. She had faced the hardships of a prospector's wife without complaining and had loved my father, willingly sharing in his quest for gold. She did not tell me so, but I feel sure that Mother had daily longed for her life among the rolling hills and woods of Missouri. Now, her grave is not in those cherished woodlands, but rather in the black depths of the mine she so abhorred.

Along the Trail, Day 4

By breaking a new path along the ridge and following Clear Creek eastward down the canyon, we have managed to avoid confronting Mr. Dumler. Two days ago we observed him on his way back to the claim. He was not alone. A man was with him. Perhaps he was bringing a doctor for Mother as he had promised to do. Father was not positive, but he thought the man was Mr. Atkinson.

It has crossed my mind to wonder if Mr. Atkinson and Mr. St. John are in league with Mr. Dumler and the three of them are planning to rob Father of his gold. I suspect Mr. Dumler covets Father's share, since Mr. Dumler lost much of his own gold while gambling in Denver City. His weakness has put us at risk from unlucky miners. By now, everyone in Denver City knows of our good fortune!

Not long ago Mr. Dumler asked Father where his cache

was hidden. Father laughed at the man's audacity. Perhaps Mr. Dumler hoped Father was no longer vigilant. After Mother became ill, Father ended his search for gold. Mr. Dumler does not, of course, know of Mother's death. I am certain Mr. Dumler is a bad man. I trust my path has crossed his for the last time.

I have considered the events of the bygone days, and I certainly have no respect for Mr. Dumler. However, in fairness, I do not think Mr. Dumler entertained at all the notion that he might do my mother harm. Contrary to the wisdom of his actions, or the outcome of his clumsy ministrations, I believe he was trying to ease her pain.

The Canyon's Mouth, Day 5

Here, in the foothills west of Denver City, I am huddled in the underwood in a natural hollow amongst some rocks with Bruno and my journal as my companions. I am guarding our gold and biding my time until Father returns with a team and a wagon. He left me the Springfield rifle, ammunition, our staples (which are secured high in a lodgepole pine), and the two small fur pelts. Bruno guards me and shall tear apart man or beast without remorse if danger comes our way. I cannot admit to fear, but even Bruno would be hard pressed in a confrontation with a cougar or a bear.

Father took Pride, his Sharps rifle, and Mother's teakwood chest with him. He plans to purchase mules or oxen, a used wagon, and enough supplies to keep us on the Smoky Hill Trail until we can take the train on east. We have heard that the Kansas Pacific Railroad is being built and is in operation as far west as Fort Harker in Kansas.

Once Father returns, we shall hide our gold in the wagon

Chapter Five — Farewell to Clear Creek Canyon

box and follow the Smoky Hill Trail from what is now Colorado Territory into Kansas. This is the shortest route across the High Plains. It is also, some say, the most hazardous of all the trails. A repetition of the warlike acts perpetrated by the Cheyenne in 1863 is not outside the realm of possibility. Bull Bear and Pawnee Killer always make the way dangerous. I would have preferred a longer and perhaps safer route, but I was not asked for an opinion. It is only a small comfort to know that the United States Cavalry sometimes provides travelers a safe escort.

Too late I have remembered my need for stockings and a toothbrush.

The Following Day

Bruno and I have eaten a small meal, and I have slept for several hours. Night is almost upon me and my faithful friend. The dark holds many demons, so I have reloaded my gun and positioned myself against the rock. The wall behind me is high enough so that a cougar cannot surprise me. How I wish Father were here, although he warned me he would not return today.

Father counseled me not to fear for his safety. However, if time passes and I am sure he has met with foul play, he said to hide the gold where it is and mark the spot. At that time I shall take my gun, and with Bruno and a pouch of gold, go into Denver City. Father said to find the office of the man who owns the *Rocky Mountain News,* William N. Byers. He and his good wife Elisabeth are Father's friends.

It WILL NOT come to this! Father shall come to no harm! While I await his return, I think wistfully of my mother and ache with loneliness. For Father the pain must be tenfold. His face reflects the sadness in his heart.

I am below the north face of the canyon. I hear the wind as it passes through the tops of the Douglas firs, the lodgepole pines, and the aspens. At first the sound is far away and then suddenly it is above me, stirring and whipping the topmost branches. Here below there is no breeze. All is calm and quiet. In spite of the wildness around me, I am comforted and rendered better able to deal with a world where pain is a part of the gift of life.

Chapter Six

Old Granger and the Smoky Hill Trail

May 31, 1867

DAWN CAME, brushing aside the night to reveal a clear sky and a brisk morning. In the safer early hours of the day I slept, only to awaken suddenly, conscious of vague fears. I determined to put such feelings aside and turned my attention to the hunger that demanded I climb the pine tree. I ate crackers and a handful of raisins while Bruno devoured a portion of dried venison.

Come midday, Bruno disappeared. He did not at once return and in time I became concerned. Therefore, I determined to search for him. I marked the hidden gold and, with my rifle, worked my way down the mountainside to the banks of Clear Creek where Bruno had repaired for a drink of water. Bruno had known sooner than I that Father was returning, for I could see him loping down the trail. I could hear the commanding bellow of Father's voice as he urged along a pair of oxen. When I first saw them, they were pulling one of those well-built Peter Schutter wagons. Father soon had made a suitable location in a grove of blue spruce and cottonwood trees.

I surveyed the ox team and wagon he said he had purchased at the Elephant Corral in Denver City. Some wag seems to have named the corral where teams and wagons are bought and sold after the beast of burden in the East Indies.

One of the oxen was as odd as the name of the place where he was bought. The lead ox, Old Granger, was a great shaggy animal and far beyond his youth. His appearance was not that of an ox at all. He had a huge round head and powerful shoulders with a matted, yellow-brown hump on his back. His horns were those of a longhorn steer, but shorter and had a peculiar downward hook. As I walked around him, scrutinizing his strange looks, he watched my every move. Only his tail and his dark eyes moved as he stood solidly on four cloven feet that were shod. What was he trying to say to me? If only he could speak!

The off-ox was smaller, a blue-gray roan named Mulberry. He was a fine animal, quite typical in looks of any ox. However, Mulberry was young and displayed the proclivities of youth. Father was warned that Mulberry was inclined to be lazy.

I inquired about the ancestry of the lead ox, and I was told he was part buffalo which was evident in the shape of his head and the hump on his back. When I asked Father

Chapter Six — Old Granger and the Smoky Hill Trail

why he was named Old Granger, I learned he had been a farm family's pet, having been raised by them.

Father was told that Old Granger was the possessor of extraordinary powers of endurance. He could pull a wagon farther and longer than an ordinary ox with little need for grass or water. With Mulberry teamed in the yoke with Old Granger, Mulberry has had no choice but to endure. Old Granger has dragged him along, shouldering the load for both of them, oblivious to Mulberry's inclination to shirk his duty.

Old Granger must live up to his reputation. Where we are going, a second yoke of oxen, or even a third, is often needed. Father said none were available for purchase at any price. These days, incoming freight from the east is very slow to reach Denver City.

I remarked to Father that mules would be faster than oxen on the trail, causing him to defend his choice. The prairie that is a part of Colorado Territory's eastern grasslands, which is only now beginning to green, has suffered a drought. He was told that a fire had burned a thirty-five mile stretch of grass from Kiowa Creek Station to the bend of the Big Sandy River. While good for the health of the prairie, the fire left little grass for grazing. Father's choice was thus the proper one. Unlike mules, oxen need less grass and water.

The burn shall take three days to cross. Old Granger and Mulberry faced this obstacle coming to Denver City. Now, instead of getting the rest they deserve, they must return over the same route. Poor beasts!

For the remainder of the day, Father and I built a hiding place for the gold above the rear axle of the wagon, using lumber bought in Denver City. We then transferred the gold. Our task was accomplished before supper.

In passing, I asked Father what he had done with

Mother's teakwood chest. He replied that he had given the chest to Mrs. Byers and charged her with offering Mother's embroidered linens to respectable young married people who come to live in growing Denver City.

Properly dated entries have been made in my journal, and I have prepared a bed for myself in the wagon box. I shall retire for the night and listen to the murmuring pines for the last time. My home in New Bordeaux becn's to me. Tomorrow Father and I shall begin our trek eastward.

June 1, 1867

This morning we spent little time completing our preparations. A cup of black coffee sustained us as we worked. While I arranged in the wagon box the goods Father had purchased in Denver City, he loaded two fifteen-gallon water barrels onto the side of the wagon.

Even though Father had plenty of gold to spend, the cost of our supplies was exorbitant. Indian activity along the trail has discouraged the bullwhackers from bringing in new goods. In spite of it, Father managed to obtain the following staples: bacon, coffee, dried beef, dried beans, sugar, flour, crackers, cornmeal, and dried apples. While all but the flour and beef were in limited quantities, even those two items were less than adequate. However, Father is knowledgeable about plants. He is able to identify those that have edible or medicinal properties. Perhaps later on we shall find ways to live off the land.

Only one purchase was, as Father put it, "an extravagance." He bought a Remington .50-caliber single-shot buffalo gun that uses an internal primer in the bullet. The gun has an unusual octagon-shaped barrel. He calls it his

"Big 50." I suspect the weight and recoil of such a weapon would be too much for most men.

Before Father yoked Old Granger and Mulberry to the wagon, he approached me with two articles. The first was a small sack tied with a stout piece of rawhide. He fastened it to my waist, hanging it from my belt in a visible manner. He instructed me not to open the sack or eat its contents. Only by cajoling was I able to induce Father to divulge that the pouch contained sugar — liberally laced with the powerfully poisonous strychnine. If ever we are at the mercy of hostiles, I am to remove my hat and show the Indians the sack. It is commonly believed the Indians shall straightaway eat the sugar, sharing it with one another, before arguing over the possession of a woman.

The thought of poisoning another human being, even a savage, did not set well with me.

The second item was a jar of butter. Someone in Denver City owned a milch cow. However, the butter was not to be eaten. Instead, Father requested me to rub small amounts into my hands and arms. He instructed me to refrain from washing myself for an extended length of time, letting the butterfat renew my rough, sunburned skin.

Tears filled my eyes, for I realized how harshly I had been treated by the elements.

Father gave me comfort, saying the damage would heal and not to fret over a circumstance that would soon pass.

When our oxen were yoked and ready for the trail, and after praying for a safe journey, Father called out to Old Granger, urging him to commence his duty. Father walked to the left of the oxen, guiding them with whip and voice. I also walked, so as not to add to their burden. Father gave me a map of the trail to help me determine the number of miles traveled each day. In my journal I shall keep a record of the terrain and where to obtain the best grass and water.

In a short time we emerged from Clear Creek Canyon and found ourselves on the flat prairie near Denver City. The snowcapped mountains all around us were very beautiful, but more than most travelers, we were aware of how dangerous they were to those who had decided to conquer their higher plateaus.

Nothing in my memory of Denver City prepared me for the sights that met my eyes as Old Granger and Mulberry pulled our wagon along Main Street in the early morning hours. When we arrived here so long ago, it was a gathering of lawless men and wanton women. In those days Denver City was only a collection of tents and log cabins. Packs of wild dogs roamed the settlement. Any animal lay in the street where it fell, ignored by everyone.

Those scenes were gone. A respectable community had replaced the helter-skelter collection of shacks. Red-brick buildings behind boardwalks bespoke of trade. Banks gave solid assurance of commerce. Main Street was wide and smooth, and the town had been laid out in city blocks. Most streets had names: Larimer, Halliday, Ferry Street. Canals carried water to nourish an abundance of grass and shade trees. Denver City becn'd to me. I would have lingered in that fair city, spending time shopping and getting acquainted with its citizens.

We progressed through the downtown almost unnoticed, past an Arapahoe Indian village, then a graveyard on a hill near the northeast edge of town. In a short time we were on the well-worn trail between Colorado Territory and Kansas.

An astonishing number of small farms and homes lined the sides of the road. They were spaced at regular intervals, marking the miles. Finally, there were no more farms or homes; we were on the open prairie.

Chapter Six — Old Granger and the Smoky Hill Trail

June 3, 1867

Upon leaving Denver City, we followed the east bank of Cherry Creek to Cherry Valley Station where we camped the first night. The grass and water were excellent. The next day we passed Piexon and a village named Parker, on our way to Ruthden Station, where we camped the second night. Water and grazing were also good at Ruthden. Today we traveled to Kiowa Creek Station where we are now camped.

We have averaged twelve miles for each day we have been on the trail. It is good to have come this far with no problems. There is plenty of water here, and the grass is turning green almost by the minute, providing forage for Old Granger and Mulberry.

Our daily routine gives our oxen the advantage and proceeds as follows. We rise with the sun each morning. After brewing a cup of coffee, Father checks the wheels of our wagon with a spanner then yokes the oxen for the day's pull. Old Granger and Mulberry pull for an hour and are then given a short break. Midway between sunup and noon we stop to rest, letting the oxen graze during the heat of the day. At this time we also eat. When the time is right, we once again yoke Old Granger and Mulberry and travel until dark.

We prefer to camp at a stage station. If we cannot, our camp is on the far side of a river or stream (if there is one), in case it rains during the night making the stream impassable.

If one of our oxen becomes ill, I pray it is not Old Granger. We shall need his stamina in the coming days. When I can, I offer him a handful of corn from our meager supply of forage.

Mulberry demands what he considers to be his due, and his small portion is always forthcoming in spite of his laziness.

Before arriving at Kiowa Creek Station, Father handed

me a bundle. The bundle contained a pair of dark-brown duck trousers, a blue-checked hickory shirt, and a felt hat with a brim wide enough to hide my face. While on the trail, I shall masquerade as a boy. My name is now Rouget. If it becomes necessary, I shall speak French. To my surprise, I found wearing trousers to my liking!

Kiowa Creek Station is a small settlement of ranches and farms, so there are people here with whom Father can converse. I find it disconcerting to have Father refer to me as Rouget. He feels compelled to explain to everyone that I am "somewhat backward," then suggests they not attempt a conversation with me unless they speak French. (No one here is French.)

The stationmaster reminds me of Mr. Dumler, although he does not resemble him in looks. I observed a curious gleam in his eyes when he inquired after Father's business. Father readily admitted he had been prospecting for gold, but he implied it was not a profitable venture.

Later this evening I discovered the stationmaster climbing into the rear of our wagon. He mumbled an incoherent explanation for his presence. Then he helped me to shift an unwieldy parfleche which I opened, "accidentally" spilling its contents. I am sure he was seeking a clue that would suggest a lie to Father's claim that he has no gold. I made sure the man was able to note exactly what we are carrying. He found no gold and left after satisfying his curiosity.

Tomorrow we begin our trek across the burn. The stationmaster was grateful the prairie fire was east of the station. Prevailing winds spared the settlement.

June 6, 1867
We are camped on the Big Sandy, a river we must cross

twice tomorrow. My mind runs upon the drudgery of the past three days. I praise God for our deliverance from the blackened desolation of the fire-scorched prairie.

The morning of June 4th we yoked Old Granger and Mulberry and headed east, knowing full well the obstacles in our path. An hour along the trail we came upon the remains of the once lush green grasslands. Blackened buffalo and blue grama grasses and smoldering buffalo dung met our gaze and filled our nostrils with an acrid smell.

This year there is a drought. In this region the prairie is as dry as tinder. When the land is parched, lightning causes the grasses to catch fire. This is a natural happening. But the prairie was not all devoured by the flames. The wildlife shall soon emerge from their underground shelters or return from their refuges beyond the reach of the fire. And with rain, grasses shall renew the scorched earth, making the prairie better than it was before the fire.

This knowledge did not help us as we made our way across the devastation. The day was long, hot, and windy. We did not reach our destination, which was Reed's Spring, a distance of twenty-one miles. Reed's Spring has a hand-dug well and a stage station, making it a much to be desired location.

Although our usual routine was broken, Old Granger and Mulberry did not fail us. When we stopped to give them rest, Father took his spade and dug up the roots of burned grass to add to the tiny bit of forage we offered them. He had doubled the amount of water we carry, which was fortuitous. The usual fifteen gallons would have been shy of our needs.

We came upon several abundant sheets of water. They becn'd to us, for we longed to quench our thirst. But according to Father, death was hidden beneath their surface. A dead deer, close by one of them, was proof of the wisdom of his words. We quickly moved on, not succumbing to their lure.

The soot from the scorched grass covered us with a sticky residue with each turn of the wagon wheels. Old Granger and Mulberry, even now, have black rings around their eyes and nostrils.

Halfway to Reed's Spring we passed Bijou Creek. We paused momentarily to quench our thirst and water the oxen before moving on. When the sun went down, we camped on the burned prairie. The night air was somewhat cooler.

Father and I were tired, but we washed ourselves the best we could with a damp rag and ate the second of our two daily meals. Father made his usual bed under the wagon. I folded back the canvas flaps on the wagon box above him and arranged my blanket.

Before saying my prayers and retiring for the night, I strolled onto the prairie and viewed the seared terrain in the darkness. It is difficult to find words to describe what I beheld. The cooled and blackened earth under my feet spread before me to the horizon. There it merged with the vast heavens into one dark arch, brilliant with countless stars. Nothing broke the silence. I could hear neither the hum of insects nor the howling of coyotes. As I gazed at the heavens, I felt the awesome presence of God.

On June 5th we camped at Reed's Spring on the west bank of the creek. Old Granger and Mulberry managed to find several patches of unburned grass to graze upon while we refilled our water kegs. We were disappointed to find the water alkaline; it was not sweet and pure like the water from the melted snow in Clear Creek. We drank it anyway and were grateful to have it.

On June 6th we traveled twelve miles to the Big Sandy River. Tonight finds us camped on the Big Bend of the Sandy. It is a haven from the heat and dust of the trail. At

Chapter Six — Old Granger and the Smoky Hill Trail

last I am able to bathe again and wash my clothes. For soap, Father gave me some buffalo gourd fruit pulp and roots. My hands, while far from soft and pretty, are beginning to heal. I long to don a dress and be myself, but this I cannot do.

June 7, 1867

During our day's progress, we came upon two bull trains headed west. The men driving the trains were the first travelers we have met. Each man had twelve yoke of oxen and was pulling a tandem wagon. They were hauling approximately eight thousand pounds each of goods. Father engaged the bullwhackers in conversation. He assured them Denver City sorely needs their wares.

The bullwhackers confirmed the rumors Father heard in Denver City of Indian attacks along the trail. He has not said so, but possibly Father now regrets his decision to follow the Smoky Hill Trail.

The men reported that spring, the season preferred by many travelers, is not the best time to cross the High Plains. This preference is understandable, for in late spring there is usually rainfall, providing plenty of water in places where a natural supply does not exist. According to the men driving the bull trains, white men often ignore the fact that winter, when the snows are deep is the better time to be on the trail. The Indians then are inclined to stay in their winter camps. But once the weather warms and there is grazing for their horses, the Indian men leave contentment behind them and ride out on raids.

This year in the middle of April, even though the Sioux and the Cheyenne have a truce with the United States government, Pawnee Killer and his Sioux warriors left Pawnee Fork just north of Fort Dodge. They attacked Lookout

Station on the Smoky Hill Trail, leaving death in their wake. At almost the same time, Roman Nose and his Cheyenne Dog Soldiers left Pawnee Fork, only to arrive at Walnut Creek where they scattered and disappeared. Several days later the stage stops east of Downer's Station were attacked. Roman Nose was responsible. The Kansas Pacific Railroad crews were harassed as well. There could be trouble in store for anyone attempting travel on the Smoky Hill Trail.

Before the bullwhackers drove on, Father gave them a map marking the best water and grass between here and Denver City. He thanked them for the information they shared with us.

June 9, 1867

In the past several days, Old Granger and Mulberry have traveled over forty miles. They are steady, uncomplaining creatures. Buying them was a stroke of good fortune.

On June 7th, the day we met the bull trains, we suffered many hours that were hot, dry, and devoid of a breeze. Buzzing insects plagued the oxen. I tied stiff stalks of dried sunflowers to the yoke above each of their heads to draw the swarms away from their eyes.

Yet there was relief from the heat, for late in the day just before we reached Hedinger's Station, we came upon several ponds of water in the Big Sandy stream bed. Father and I went for a swim. For a brief time, the sadness left him. Perhaps his grief over Mother's death is beginning to heal.

There was a cave at Hedinger's Station. While Father visited with the stationmaster, I crept into its cool, dark recess and slept. While I slept, I dreamed I was once again under the murmuring pines along Clear Creek. I could hear the wind whispering my name. When I awoke, I was certain someone as lonely as I am had called to me.

The next day, June 8th, we traveled to Hogan Station. The trail was smooth and level along the north bank of the Big Sandy. The deer, buffalo, and antelope were all around us in great herds. The land was teeming with smaller creatures as well. Overhead a red-shouldered hawk circled in search of his morning meal, perhaps a small rodent.

That night we camped on the prairie near Hogan Spring. Here the land was not devastated by the drought. During the night, the air was thick with the smell of lightning, and the sound of thunder rolled menacingly overhead. Blinding bolts split the sky, but not a drop of rain fell to the ground.

Today, June 9th, we awoke to a cool breeze that was coming our way from the mountains. The day was bright with sunshine, and I enjoyed the passing hours as I walked beside our oxen. Most of the time, behind us the Rockies' high peaks were still visible and not lost in a haze.

I have tried, and failed, to summon the courage to ask Father if he is worried that with the exception of the two bull trains, we have met no fellow travelers. I am certain it would have been safer to follow the Santa Fe Trail.

June 10, 1867

We are camped at Connell Creek Station on the east bank of the Sandy, having crossed it before making our location. The land is not level here, but the grass and water are adequate. The station is situated on the west side of the creek and is nothing more than a hole, resembling a cave. At this point Connell Creek flows down from the north and into the Big Sandy.

To reach the station, we were forced to follow the incline

first down and then up the other side of the draw. The incline was steep, but it was not too difficult for Old Granger to negotiate. Father chained the back wheels so they would not turn and Old Granger dragged the wagon by himself. Mulberry did not pull his share of the load. Father was most annoyed with him! Mulberry, of course, was unrepentant. I fear he shall find himself sold at the first opportunity.

There is little to break the monotony of our days. What occurs is sometimes distressing to witness. Today on a rise stood a lone bull buffalo with arrow shafts bristling in his sides and hump. Fate had allowed him to escape the final assault of a hunt. Overhead birds of prey drifted, held aloft by air currents. They were waiting for the inevitable to happen. As Father and I watched, the buffalo slowly sank to his knees where he remained for several minutes. Then suddenly, with one agonized bellow, he rolled to the ground where he quivered for a moment, then died.

Why did I feel such sadness to see him die? There are millions of the great beasts. They frequently blacken the horizon. Of what possible significance is one buffalo?

June 11, 1867

Tonight we are camped at Grady's Station. There is good grass here, but the water is alkaline and the oxen dislike it.

Once again, the station is only a cave cut into the bank of a stream. The stationmaster is a recluse; he does not readily converse with passersby. We obtained no news from him. We are in the dark as to conditions farther down the trail.

Today Mulberry was willing to pull his share of the load. Perhaps he shall regain Father's good will.

A cool breeze from the mountains takes the edge off the heat we endured all day. The snowcapped peaks are still

Chapter Six — Old Granger and the Smoky Hill Trail

visible, but from here they show only a fraction of their size.

I wonder how many men who came west seeking gold in the Rocky Mountains went on to find it in paying quantities? A mere handful, I'll wager. For those who did strike it rich, the price they paid for success was often far too high.

Understand this: I do not disparage gold, for I see no virtue in poverty. Poverty makes one a beggar. For myself, I seek another kind of wealth. I prefer the wealth that comes from belonging to a family and having meaningful work to do. These riches are within the purview of any man or woman.

June 12, 1867

We left Grady's Station soon after sunrise and did not see its unfriendly stationmaster. What little we could pry from him last evening let us know he shall soon be departing for Denver City, leaving his station unoccupied.

When we reached Dubois Station, we found it to be deserted. It has not suffered in an Indian raid. We are unable to explain the situation.

Tonight we have made our location on the far bank of the Big Sandy. The river water again is alkaline, as is the water in the hand-dug well nearby. Like it or not, we must drink it.

Before dark Father dismantled the heavy, muslin-like cover over the bows of our wagon. This done, he also removed the bows, which were fastened to the sides of the wagon box. These he discarded, as it was impossible to take them with us. He then tied the cover back over our load, making it even with the sides. He has done this to make us less visible on the trail, for we cannot ignore the fact that we have seen evidence of hostiles.

The next two days shall be difficult. Tomorrow we face over twenty-four miles of desolation. Our map indicates the possibility of a single water hole early on. Thereafter, we shall depend upon the water we carry with us.

Tonight we did not light a campfire. The farther east we go, the more uneasy Father becomes. Increasingly, I too feel the tension. Early in the day as I walked beside Old Granger and Mulberry, I noticed the sky was devoid of birds. Even the prairie falcon that frequents the draws and small rock canyons hereabouts was not to be seen. The sharp-tailed grouse was also hiding. Most ominous of all, tonight the coyotes are quiet, a sure indication of the presence of Indians.

We have been on the trail for twelve days and have come almost one hundred forty miles, less than a third of the distance to the train at Fort Harker. Here at Dubois Station the trail divides, the southern branch leading to Fort Lyon. We shall continue to follow the Smoky Hill Trail, pressing on east sixty more miles and crossing into Kansas with Fort Wallace in mind as a refuge. We are hoping the Fort shall afford us sanctuary until such time the trail becomes safe.

It is possible that today was my last glimpse of the Rockies. In the southwest loomed Pikes Peak. Its spectacular summit is always snowcapped and therefore visible. Toward evening I rode in the wagon box, looking back at the cloud-topped range, now so diminished in size. All the while I was occupied with thoughts of my mother. As it grew dark, with a heavy heart, I watched the resplendently beautiful mountain fade from my view.

Chapter Seven

Biding Time

7:30 PM, July 5, 1967

JULIA RUBBED HER eyes and stretched, arching her tired back. She marked her place and closed Yvette's journal. "I wish I could know Yvette," she murmured.

Chris had a faraway look in his eyes. "Me, too. I wonder what she looked like. She didn't describe herself. She must have been pretty strong to have carried a backpack loaded with gold."

"Maybe she looked like you, Julia," Chris added, giving Julia a quick glance. "I'd be willing to bet she was beautiful!"

Julia looked startled. "Well, I wouldn't know about that. Yvette wrote about Pierre's gold and about her life, which was lonely. I don't see how you can compare her to me. It's odd you think I might look like Yvette."

"Yvette had a difficult youth," Chris noted. "Pierre's obsession with gold had deprived her of a normal relationship with her friends and family."

Julia nodded and brushed a damp strand of hair away from her forehead.

Chris pushed back his chair concluding, "Well, tonight we're not going to solve the mystery of where the gold was buried. Let's take my pickup into town and get a burger and a malt." He checked the contents of his billfold.

"It's my treat. August is paying me to plow at night. He couldn't get anyone to turn the wheat stubble after the custom cutter moved on. I wanted to do it as a favor, but he wouldn't hear of it."

Julia opened her book bag, slipped the journal inside, and buckled the straps.

"Okay, thanks! I'm saving my money for college."

"Well, I am too," answered Chris, "but it's no fun squeezing every penny 'til it squeaks. Besides, time gets away. I want to buy you a burger and a malt *now!*"

Julia recalled Matt's letter. The possibility that Chris might be drafted was frequently in her thoughts, too.

"Are your folks able to send you to college?" she asked. "Mine don't have a prayer of sending me. What'll you study?"

Chris had never confided his own ambitions to anyone, and he was surprised to hear himself say, "I'd like to attend the agricultural college at Manhattan."

Julia acknowledged that it was a good school.

Chris shrugged. "But asking my folks to foot the bill for a college education is like asking for the moon. Dad owes the bank for several years of bad crops. I suspect he's in debt up to his ears."

Julia pondered both their situations. "Something will work out. It always does."

"It's really strange," said Julia, changing the subject back to Yvette. "I feel as if I'm Yvette and have come back to the Fort a hundred years later, determined to settle the fate of my father's gold!"

Chapter Seven — Biding Time

Chris tousled Julia's curls, teasing her, "Perhaps you do resemble Yvette, but I like girls with short hair. All my girlfriends have had short hair!"

Julia made a face at Chris. "I've heard about your girlfriends! You even have good old Miss Bloxham eating out of your hand. There isn't a female for miles around that doesn't love you! Well, you won't find me breaking down your door!"

With this declaration Julia rose, tucked the book bag under her arm, and started to leave.

As Chris got up, he remarked, "Probably not today."

But Julia didn't hear his comment.

Chris locked the front door as they left, and Old Major rose to his feet from his comfortable position under the window. He stretched and followed them down the steps, confident that Julia would go to the tool shed, fill his food bowl, and freshen his drinking water before she left the Fort for the day.

Neither Julia nor Chris noticed that Old Major, glancing back and forth to each of them, seemed to be patiently waiting for something more to happen.

Chapter Eight

Much to Think About

July 6-9, 1967

FOR THE NEXT three days Julia and Chris had no time to spend together. They both had to work full shifts, which forced them to delay reading more of Yvette's journal. Chris had even less time than Julia. His workday was only half over when he left the Fort at five o'clock.

Every evening after one of Mrs. Janning's wonderful suppers — home baked bread, roast beef, potatoes and gravy, or any other of her tasty farm meals — Chris would feed and groom the horses, then hook August's one-way disk plow to his John Deere 4020 row-crop tractor and head for the wheat field to turn August's wheat stubble until midnight. The sense of high adventure Chris had felt earlier in the week, thinking about the lost gold, quickly succumbed to fatigue.

Chapter Eight — Much to Think About

On Sunday, July 9th, Julia was alone. Chris had gone home to visit his family, and she had decided to spend the afternoon back at the Fort pursuing the clues in Yvette's riddle. After attending Mass together, Jennifer drove Julia to the Fort and dropped her off in the parking lot at one o'clock. She promised to return at five to take Julia home.

As Julia entered the Tourist Center, she observed several visitors viewing a miniature replica of Fort Hays' buildings and grounds. The replica was a relief map of the garrison, made to scale. When they moved on, Julia took their place at the glass case and examined the Fort's early layout, thinking . . . *My great-great grandfather hid his gold somewhere on the grounds of this Fort. I plan to find it, if it's the last thing I ever do!*

> *Upon the Fourth a fortnight past,*
> *The fortress sleeps.*
> *The hands at five, due west.*
> *As heaven's light appears at dawn,*
> *Creeps downward, brings to notice*
> *Earth that welcomes gold returned to home.*

Julia whispered the riddle to herself several times, but nothing startling came to mind. Then she began to focus her attention on the replica of the house on Officers Row where she and Chris had been reading Yvette's journal. Something about the house drew her attention. Staring at the doll-like structure, she suddenly remembered the ornate pendulum clock on the west parlor wall. The harvest scene that was painted in golden tints and earth tones on the clock's glass door was also a picture of a rosy sunrise behind distant hills.

Julia hurried to the phone in the employees' lounge and called Jennifer at home. Jennifer confirmed Julia's recollection that the clock had belonged to Major Alfred Gibbs, the Fort's Commanding Officer in 1867.

Julia felt her efforts were beginning to pay off. The riddle inferred the clock, she reasoned. The riddle also referred to the dawn and to the light that appeared with the beginning of the day. *It's a start*, she said to herself.

Julia went to the supply room for a pencil and a pad of paper; then with Jennifer's permission, she took the key to the house on Officers Row and left the Center. Old Major joined her as she walked along the boardwalk. He barked joyfully at the prospect of having her all to himself.

Julia sat on the porch with Old Major beside her. *What facts fit the riddle?* she asked herself. She was concentrating, trying to penetrate the web of words to find a clear picture. She made notes on the pad of paper to help her think.

> *sleep (not daytime)*   *18th day of July*
> *earth*   *light creeps down*
> *time — must be 5:00 AM — sun shining at 5:00 PM*
> *clock?*   *sunrise — dawn*   *fortress — location?*
>   *Why is "due west" important?*

Well, there is the date to consider, she thought, as she drew a line under "18th day of July." The riddle also mentioned "sleep." So whatever took place might have happened before the sun came up on July 18th. The riddle assigned a specific time, *five* o'clock. And a direction: *due west*. And it referred to the sunrise.

The clock was now on the west wall of the parlor, though Jennifer was not sure if that was where it had been placed by Major Gibbs.

Julia's brow was furrowed and insight escaped her. After a time, she rose to her feet and walked to the front door. Old Major, knowing he could not follow her into the house, settled under the window in the company of a dragonfly.

Julia entered the house and locked the door behind her. She walked across the parlor and stood in front of the clock. After scrutinizing the timepiece, she reached up, then opened the glass door and set the pendulum swinging with a rhythmic *tick-tock*. She moved the hour hand to the numeral five, the minute hand to twelve.

Chapter Eight — Much to Think About

"Five o'clock," she said as the clock chimed five times. "*The hands at five, due west.*"

Then Julia realized that the wall holding the clock's shelf was not aligned due west. The house had been built at an angle. The wall was somewhat northwest. That doesn't fit the riddle thought Julia, feeling frustrated. Besides, how can the rising and expanding light that comes with dawn also creep downward?

She folded the piece of paper that held her notes and tucked it into her pocket. She locked the door to the house on Officers Row and returned the key to Jennifer's office, then told Old Major "Good-bye." At five o'clock Jennifer arrived to take her home.

Julia knew she had failed once again. She was as baffled by the riddle as any of her relatives who had tried to find Pierre's gold.

Chapter Nine

Bad News

July 10, 1967

ON MONDAY MORNING, only minutes after Julia had escorted a family from Kansas City around the premises, she noticed her parents' station wagon in the parking lot. Julia's mother, an older version of Julia, was a hard-working farmer's wife who seldom came to town alone. Mr. Simmons was a capable and deliberate man with graying brown hair and glasses; and he almost never acted on impulse. Julia knew that her folks' appearance at the Fort was not a social call.

She hurried to the rear door of the Center. As soon as she entered the building, she saw her parents. Her mother was obviously grieving, and Julia's father was trying to comfort her.

Chapter Nine — Bad News

Chris and Jennifer, poring over a letter, stood apart from the Simmons. Their faces were etched with concern. Julia's mother covered her mouth with one hand, trying to suppress her sobs, when she saw her daughter.

For a moment Julia did not comprehend the situation. And then she understood.

"*NO!*" she screamed, and ran from the building.

The family from Kansas City had retired to the picnic area and were enjoying sandwiches and iced tea in the sparse shade of several Siberian elms. They looked up in time to see Julia's anguished tear-stained face. Their eyes followed her, and they saw her disappear behind the guardhouse. They glanced helplessly at each other, knowing there was nothing they could do.

Sobs racked Julia's body. She leaned her forehead against the rough limestone building.

Before long, she heard Chris's voice. It took several seconds for the meaning of his words to penetrate her thoughts.

"He's *not dead*, Julia!"

Julia was still crying and was so upset that she was unable to stop.

"He's not dead . . . but he's lost his right leg."

Julia's body was quivering uncontrollably as she turned to face Chris.

"Your father talked to Matt on the telephone this morning. He's in Hawaii. He'll soon be coming home."

Julia did not respond and continued to sob.

"Hey!" Chris said forcefully. "Matt is a survivor. He can deal with this! My father's Army buddy lost a leg in World War II fighting at the Battle of the Bulge. He was outfitted with an artificial leg. He limps when he's tired, but he recovered from his injuries. Later on he got married and entered college on the GI Bill. He put his life back together. Matt can too."

Julia shook her head angrily. "Where are the people responsible for what happened to my brother? Who decided he was expendable? I hate them! I want to tell them how much I hate them! Matt was a whole person when he left home."

Chris took a step toward Julia.

"It won't change anything, Julia. All you'll do is allow the hate to devour you."

"He had a one-year tour of duty," sobbed Julia. "His time was almost up!"

She turned her back to Chris. Once again she began to cry, but this time her tears were a silent, steady display of grief that rolled in torrents down her face.

"When you see Matt again, you'll feel better," said Chris. "Everything will work out. That's a promise."

Julia turned to face Chris, her voice soft and wavering.

"I'm not crying only for Matt. History is nothing more than an unconscionable record of battles between people who never seem to be able to find an alternative to war.

"Vietnam hangs like a black cloud over both our lives. Someday will I be crying for *you*?"

Julia covered her face with her hands, realizing she had voiced her greatest fear. Her hands dropped away from her face, and Chris lifted her chin and kissed her. Putting his arms around her, he held her close until the tears and sobs had stopped.

Later that evening, after Julia's parents had gone home, Julia and Chris went for a walk along Big Creek where Chris kissed Julia again and tried to convince her not to lose hope. He assured her that somehow Matt would resolve what had happened to him in Vietnam. His letter stated he wanted to live just one day at a time.

Chris was determined that the threatening shadow of war, at least for the time being, would not cloud their lives unless they allowed it.

Chapter Ten

All in a Day's Work

July 11-13, 1967

ON TUESDAY, JULY 11th, an element of unspoken sadness permeated the Fort. Matt's loss had affected others besides Julia and Chris. Jennifer had known Matt all his life and she, too, was grieving for him.

To Julia, it was a tedious day, and she had difficulty keeping her mind on her work. Most of her thoughts concerned her brother. It was a struggle for her to focus on anything other than Matt's injury.

Julia was also waiting, somewhat impatiently, for an opportunity to be alone with Chris. But she knew that until the coming weekend, Chris was working sixteen-hour days. They managed only to share their lunch breaks.

It was Old Major who provided diversion for Julia. By the time the usual activity and what turned out to be unexpected excitement of the afternoon was over, much of the gloom at the Fort had lifted.

Late that day, a four-year-old boy had wandered into the buffalo pasture adjacent to the Fort. As the child and his parents were viewing the small herd of American bison grazing in the pasture along Big Creek, the parents noticed a flat tire on the family's car. During the time they were changing the tire, the little boy decided to take a closer look at the newborn buffalo calf inside the barbed-wire fence enclosure. Too young to read the signs that said, "DANGER, KEEP OUT," he crawled beneath the fence and commenced walking across the rugged grass, headed toward the northeast corner where the herd was clustered in the shade of the cottonwood trees.

When it was all over, no one was certain where she came from, but suddenly an angry cow, whose calf had died, was facing the boy. She stood in the dry grass where the herd's churning hooves had reduced the soil to a grayish powder. Her bloodshot eyes glittered as her head lowered almost to the ground; her breath whiffled and puffed up clouds of dust; she pawed the ground with her right hoof as her rib cage heaved with rage.

The boy had stopped walking, for fear had made him motionless. He uttered one word, *"Mama!"*

At that moment, Old Major ducked under the fence and trotted to the center of the pasture. He ignored the boy. His eyes were on the angry buffalo cow. His teeth were bared and the hair on the scruff of his neck stood straight up; his growl was the challenge of an animal prepared to fight to the death.

At once, the enraged cow turned her attention to Old Major and the battle began. The cow tried her best to hook her adversary with her horns, but Old Major dodged her thrust and circled her as he nipped at her heels, twirling her around and around. All the while, he was working his way toward the fence. With remarkable tactical skill, he kept the cow at bay until the boy's parents could snatch their child to safety.

Chapter Ten — All in a Day's Work

Once the boy was rescued, Old Major ducked under the fence and beat a hasty retreat. His tongue dangled from his mouth in exhaustion. But his eyes gleamed with the thrill of victory.

The boy's parents were shaken by the experience. They quickly finished changing their tire and went to look for the courageous black dog. Julia introduced them to Old Major.

After his skirmish, Old Major had joined Julia and Jennifer who were sitting under the elms in the picnic area. They were astonished at the rescue related by the boy's parents. Old Major seemed pleased to meet the family and wagged his tail with gusto.

Someone called the *Daily News* with the story, and on Wednesday Old Major's picture was in the local paper, making him a hero. Julia was busy dealing with Old Major's admirers, and for a short time she forgot her grief.

Jennifer jokingly told everyone that now she was positive Old Major was Custer's ghost for only Custer would be gutsy enough to confront an infuriated buffalo! But Old Major acted as if this was all in a day's work.

Chapter Eleven

Back to an Age Long Gone

July 14, 1967

BY THE 14TH, Julia had a feeling she was running out of time. Matt would be coming home in a matter of weeks, and as yet, the mystery of Pierre's gold was unsolved. She was more determined than ever to discover any glimmer of information that might be revealed in the journal.

After work on Friday, Julia and Chris stopped by Jennifer's office and asked for the key to the house on Officers Row. As Jennifer took the key from her desk, her eyes spoke volumes. She had not failed to notice Julia's and Chris's changed relationship.

Julia and Chris strolled hand in hand across the grass toward

Chapter Eleven — Back to an Age Long Gone

Officers Row. Old Major followed them, content to be with his two favorite people. As they opened the door to the house, Old Major, instead of waiting for them on the porch, shoved his way inside. He yelped as the book bag, containing Yvette's journal, was unceremoniously dropped on his head, and he found himself tangled in the couple's embrace. After circling around them for several minutes, asking for their attention and being ignored, Old Major shoved his way between their knees, effectively ending their special moment. With obvious irritation, Julia grabbed Old Major by his collar, ordered him outside, and told him to lie down under the window.

"Three's a crowd!" she told him.

Chris's laughter brought a wry grin to Julia's face.

The hallway of the house was stifling, but Julia and Chris again stood in the heat with their arms around each other, enjoying their brief moment of privacy. After several minutes Julia remarked, "It's hot in here! Let's open the windows and get a bit of the breeze."

They released each other and Julia reached down and picked up her book bag. Chris, once again, unlatched and raised the window sashes. A welcome breath of fresh air, pungent with the scent of plowed earth, replaced the room's stale atmosphere.

"Do you want me to read this time?"

"No," answered Julia. "It's a bit uncanny. When I read the journal, I can feel Yvette's personality. It's as if I'm Yvette!"

They took their places at the table. Julia removed the marker from the journal. "Here's where I stopped. Pierre and Yvette were camped at Dubois Station. Pierre had decided to try to reach Fort Wallace."

Chapter Twelve

Cheyenne Wells Station

June 13, 1867

WE BROKE CAMP today just before dawn and risked a small fire to make our morning coffee. Father filled our water barrels; then he cut the hay he found in a draw and piled it on top of our wagon. It is prudent to assure forage for Old Granger and Mulberry, although here the drought has been less severe. The day turned hot and windy and the sun was merciless. Late in the afternoon, once again I rode in the back of the wagon and this time I watched Pikes Peak disappear forever below the horizon.

The next stage stop is Cheyenne Wells Station, more

Chapter Twelve — Cheyenne Wells Station

than a two-day trek. Since today we did not reach our destination, tonight we have camped on the prairie. We decided not to build a campfire. Its glow would be visible for miles. I think we are alone out here. It comforts me to hear the coyotes howling.

June 18, 1867

We are finally at Cheyenne Wells Station. For the past several days, Father's life has hung by a delicate thread. He suffered a rattlesnake bite on his leg while extricating our wagon from a difficulty. Until today, I could not be certain he would live.

Two misfortunes occurred after leaving Dubois Station. The tale must be told from the beginning.

Before noon on June 14th, we rested and gave forage to Old Granger and Mulberry. It was I who first noticed Old Granger's peculiar behavior. He refused to graze and tossed his head about as he rolled his eyes and stamped the ground with one forefoot.

Mulberry was not as agitated as Old Granger and commenced grazing. From time to time Mulberry would raise his head and look in a southeasterly direction.

Pride and Bruno were also alert; they climbed to a rise and stood like statues, looking east and south.

The reaction of our animals to something we had not yet discerned caused Father and me to suspect other people were in our vicinity. It occurred to us that perhaps Mr. Dumler and his cohorts were following our trail, hoping to steal Father's gold. We quickly dismissed the thought, but our animals continued to direct their attention to the southeast.

Father decided to be cautious, so it was prudent to have Mulberry and Old Granger pull the wagon off the trail. He directed them to a small box canyon several hundred feet to the south. He did this without checking the dimensions of the canyon.

After Father chained the wheels, our oxen dragged the wagon down an incline and through a narrow neck with high rock walls on either side. Once the wagon was hidden, Father took his rifle and scouted the horizon from the rock ridge over our heads. His vigil was rewarded by the sight of a dust trail moving to the southeast. It soon disappeared, leaving the plains without evidence of human presence.

Since there was grass in the canyon, we unhitched Old Granger and Mulberry, allowing them to graze. Then we waited for three hours. When we determined it was safe to return to the trail, we yoked our oxen and tried to turn the wagon around. It was a useless exercise. The space at the bottom of the canyon was not wide enough to allow the maneuver.

This, however, was not an insurmountable problem. Father unchained Old Granger and Mulberry from the wagon box and led them to the back. He hooked the chains to the rear axle and fastened them to the yoke. I took the whip and Father took hold of the wagon tongue to steer. Old Granger and Mulberry easily pulled the wagon backward out of the canyon and onto level ground.

Suddenly, we heard a rending crash! The sound of splintering wood was disconcerting. Father said something angrily in French that I did not comprehend. The wheel behind Old Granger had dropped into a deep crevice in the exposed bedrock and was tightly wedged. Old Granger, with his mighty strength, continued to pull. The axle was made of sturdy white oak, but he snapped it as easily as if it had been a twig. Fortunately, I was able to stop him before he had damaged it beyond repair. Then he placidly chewed his cud while Father and I assessed the damage.

Chapter Twelve — Cheyenne Wells Station

Mulberry's head was lowered. He seemed to deny any responsibility for our predicament, which was true. I saw the yoke shift on his neck! It was Old Granger alone who made an effort to pull. I must state it bluntly: Mulberry had once again shirked his duty.

We were still a distance away from Cheyenne Wells Station. It was imperative we arrive there before our water supply was depleted.

To repair the damage, Father placed a large stone under the break. By using an oak plank he had stored under the wagon for emergencies, he was able to lever the axle into alignment. While Father held the broken ends together, I crawled under the axle. With little trouble, I wrapped it in a length of chain and hooked the chain at each end, whereupon Father lowered his lever, dropping the weight onto the chain. Father used a mattock to break the rock around the wedged wheel, and we pulled free.

This was the first misfortune.

The second mishap was a true disaster and not easily remedied. It happened as Old Granger and Mulberry were properly yoked and we were preparing to return to the trail. Father reached down to retrieve the plank he had thrown to one side. As he leaned over we both heard that rustling sound, like the wind in the grass. Father dropped the board he had lifted just as a prairie rattlesnake's fangs found their mark. The snake's fangs penetrated Father's trousers and pierced the ankle above his left boot. The mattock that was still in Father's hand came crashing down. It was an accurate blow and in an instant the snake was dead, whereupon Father kicked its body into some tall grass.

Father could not easily tend the wound, and my assistance was required. First, he removed his left boot and cut away the leg of his trousers. Then he gave me his knife and told me to scrape the puncture until it bled freely. I used my mouth to suck the deadly venom. This done, we needed ammonia to aid the cure. Having none, I made a poultice using the soil from a nearby urine-soaked buffalo wallow and tied it tightly over the bite. Through it all father remained calm.

Once the wound was dressed, Father climbed into the back of the wagon where he leaned against a parfleche. When he was comfortable, I led Old Granger and Mulberry back to the trail and began the long walk to Cheyenne Wells Station. No doubt Pride sensed my fear, for his primal howl beseeched the Fates to be kind to us in the coming ordeal.

Once we were back on the trail, it took twenty grueling hours to reach the station. The distance proved to be a test for all of us. I set Mulberry and Old Granger their pace, which was much slower than I would have preferred. Except for water breaks from our supply, I kept them moving. Thanks to Providence, the broken axle held together. The moon aided us with its luminous glow as we traveled throughout the night.

God's blessings on Old Granger! His endurance was beyond expectation. After fifteen hours, I unyoked Mulberry and tied him to the rear of the wagon to trail behind, or he would have faltered. From then on, Old Granger pulled the wagon alone.

By now, Bruno was exhausted. I allowed him to ride in the wagon with Father. Evidently Pride's wild heredity had enabled him to persevere. Fatigue was foreign to his nature.

When I looked to see how Father was faring, I found him in pain, for his leg was swollen. I tried to remain calm as I offered Father a drink of water before we drove on, every turn of the wheels taking us closer to Cheyenne Wells Station.

At noon the next day, June 15th, I guided Old Granger

Chapter Twelve — Cheyenne Wells Station

along the ridge above the valley of the Big Sandy River. My hopes for assistance were high as I looked down on the barn, the livestock corral, and the station.

Those hopes were soon dashed. No smoke emerged from the chimney on the frame building. There were no horses or mules in the barn or the corral. The station had been abandoned.

In spite of my disappointment at finding no person who could lend us a helping hand, all was not lost. The station offered outstanding defense possibilities. It was situated halfway up an incline on a cliff and was located next to a cave. The vista gave an excellent view of the prairie, which sloped eastward a considerable distance, before dropping into a deep ravine that followed the riverbed. These were the headwaters of the Smoky Hill River. I assessed the location and decided it would make a good camp until Father was well enough to travel.

I climbed down from the driver's seat and walked to the rear of the wagon, saying to Father that Cheyenne Wells Station was below us. I remarked that God had treated us kindly, for the broken axle, with its repair, was intact. I could see relief in Father's eyes, and I knew his concern was not for himself, but for me. I reassured him with a smile and returned to the task at hand.

The trail followed a gentle slope into the valley. I considered carefully before I chained the rear wheels, for I recalled the monumental feat of endurance already achieved by Old Granger. I feared I might tax him beyond his limit. But at last I admitted that my woman's body no doubt lacked the stamina to hold the hand brake on such a long descent. Sadly, I could see no way around it. Reluctantly, I attached the chain so that the wheels would not turn, and Old Granger bowed his enormous head and strained forward, putting his great strength to the undertaking.

On the horizon, storm clouds were gathering as Old Granger pulled the wagon into the cave. There was but a hairbreadth of room for him to maneuver. His nose was against the wall, but the wagon was inside the cave.

By the time Old Granger was free of his yoke, there was a downpour. As he turned around, preparing to leave the cave, he squeezed his huge body between the wall of the cave and the wagon. I noticed long strands of the matted hair on his hump that had caught in crevices of the rock.

Once outside the cave, Old Granger moved to Mulberry's side. Both stood with lowered heads, their rumps to the wind and rain, riding out the storm.

When the sky cleared, I led the oxen down the slope to the banks of the Smoky Hill River where they might quench their thirst. Then I led them to the barn, where I piled sweet-smelling prairie hay in front of them. I carried armloads of the hay into the cave and filled the wagon box, lastly covering the piles with blankets for Father to sleep upon. I placed hay for my own bed under the wagon, leaving the task of carrying our belongings into the station for the morrow.

The next several days were so agonizing for Father it made my heart ache. Nothing I did gave him comfort. He needed to be inside the station, but I could not lift him, and he could not walk. In fact, he found the pain of being touched unbearable. The snake must have unleashed considerable venom. The bite area was numb, and Father's face tingled, especially around his mouth. He was subject to short, violent fits of retching, which resulted in a severe nose bleed. He could not eat, and I despaired when he refused a sip of water.

Nevertheless, today Father filled my heart with sunshine by smiling at me and assuring me he would live.

Chapter Twelve — Cheyenne Wells Station

July 1, 1867

It has been over two weeks since Father suffered the snakebite. His condition shows improvement with each passing day. He is still not well, but I think perhaps the worst is over.

A week ago Father left the cave. He used two chairs for crutches and hobbled to the station, where he lowered himself onto the bed. His brow was beaded with sweat, and I was aware of the effort the exercise had required.

I unwrapped the mud dressing on Father's leg and cleansed the wound, leaving it open to the air. The bite area was red and raw, but it did not look putrescent. Afterward, he bathed and changed into clean clothes.

For our evening meal I prepared a passenger pigeon I had snared in the rafters of the barn. I was pleased to be able to offer Father such exquisite fare.

While Father ate his supper, I dug up the roots of white polygala, a prairie wildflower, and a proven remedy for snakebite. As I washed, dried, then pounded the roots of the plant into a moist pulp to dress Father's wound, I asked if he had been afraid he would die. He replied that while the possibility of death had crossed his mind, he had not dwelled upon it. If it was his time, he observed, he could die as well as the next man.

July 2, 1867

Of late, Father's gold has been the least of my concerns. But today an incident occurred which made it foremost in my mind.

This morning, just before noon, a stage from Denver City arrived in Cheyenne Wells. Its passengers, two engineers associated with the building of the railroad, were on their way to Fort Wallace to see Colonel Greenwood, the railroad's chief engineer. The men cited reports of Indian attacks, and urged us to abandon our belongings and take the stage with them to Fort Wallace.

Father refused, however, for he would never abandon his gold; he insisted upon remaining at the station until he could effect proper repairs to his wagon.

The men left after a noon meal and had to travel thirty-six miles, crossing over the Kansas border after dark. They promised to alert the Cavalry of our plight.

July 4, 1867

Today is Independence Day! Our country has been free of British rule for ninety-two years. It would be a grand occasion to celebrate, but we have more pressing matters.

Toward evening, due east of us I spied horses headed our way. I had just brought three buckets of water up the hill from a well on the Smoky when a platoon of twenty cavalrymen rode into Cheyenne Wells.

Father struggled to his feet and met them at the door of the station. He introduced me as Rouget to the Lieutenant in charge of the men. When Father told the Lieutenant that I speak French, he did not grasp the meaning of Father's statement. Thinking both Father and me to be more proficient in the French language than in English, the Lieutenant called back to the ranks and brought forward a black-haired, black-eyed young man. He was dressed in a slouch hat, knee-high black boots, and a dark blue uniform of yellow-trimmed kersey. Private Andre Lesseps spoke French, and asked us how he could be of service.

Upon hearing our story, the Lieutenant assigned a detail. Private Lesseps, an officer, and two others were ordered to

Chapter Twelve — Cheyenne Wells Station

stay behind and help us repair the axle on our wagon. They were also to protect us until we reached Fort Wallace. After watering their horses, the rest of the platoon left to complete its patrol.

Private Lesseps is a fine man and highly educated. His father is a well-to-do shipbuilder, originally from Quebec. For an unknown reason, several months before Private Lesseps was born, the father took his family to Boston. Consequently, Private Lesseps is a citizen of this country. He also shared with us the fact that he is not a newcomer to the military. He served the Northern cause during the Civil War under the command of General Custer. By all accounts, Private Lesseps has lived a dangerous life for someone so young!

Private Lesseps was quick to tell us that on July 3rd, the stagecoach transporting the two railroad engineers was attacked by Indians west of Pond Creek. Both men and the driver were wounded. I think Father was sorry he was not there to help defend the stage. It was unfortunate the men found themselves under attack, but defending them was not Father's responsibility. He should not blame himself for what happened.

July 5, 1867

Early this morning, July 5th, Private Lesseps offered to fix the broken axle. I was delighted! We collected the tools he would need and went to the cave. It was not until Private Lesseps had picked up a hand auger, a mallet, and several wooden pegs and had started to crawl under the wagon that I remembered the hidden gold! In a panic, I took his place, losing my hat in the process and exposing my long hair. I quickly covered my head again, but Private Lesseps had seen me. His surprise was obvious. Upon observing my true gender all he could find to say was, "Lordy!"

I am afraid I was less than civil to Private Lesseps. I told him I intended to fix the axle myself and kicked him from beneath the wagon. He assisted me by levering the broken ends of the shaft into alignment. I neatly pegged the splintered pieces and wrapped the chain again, reinforcing the repair. I was unable to tell if Private Lesseps had seen the hidden compartment. However, he did not seem curious about the underside of the wagon.

Private Lesseps now spends a large portion of his time hovering close to me. I am most annoyed. I no longer enjoy the comfort of being sometimes alone. I have requested him to please be merciful and respect my privacy. I also asked him to keep my secret. This he solemnly promised to do.

July 6, 1867

Last night our four-man detachment was encamped in the open. The threat of Indians prevented us from building a fire, so for the first time since our arrival at Cheyenne Wells, we were denied the luxury of hot food.

I overheard one of the men tell Private Lesseps it was a miracle that the Cheyenne and the Sioux had not discovered Father and me. The man had grisly stories to tell. As Private Lesseps listened to his companion, he glanced in my direction and seemed uneasy.

Today we were up before dawn, preparing to leave for Fort Wallace. I gathered an abundance of white polygala roots and dressed Father's wound. He was in pain, but he walked to the wagon unassisted. I decided to spoil Bruno and Pride. I allowed them to ride in the wagon box with Father.

Chapter Twelve — Cheyenne Wells Station

Before I yoked Old Granger and Mulberry, Private Lesseps entered the station with two cups of hot coffee. I am not sure how this was managed, for I was not aware of a fire. I smiled and told him he had saved my life, which seemed to please him. At the same time, he gave me a loaded Colt handgun. If we are overcome by hostiles, I am to save two bullets, one for myself and one for Father. I shall say no more about the gun.

I am still wearing the sack of poisoned sugar. When I mentioned the sugar, Private Lesseps counseled me to wear the sack, but not depend upon it.

Before Private Lesseps left to rejoin the men, he asked me to call him Andre. He said he had not had anyone call him by his given name for a very long time.

We were soon on the trail, and after many hours of wending our way through treacherous canyons, we reached a place near the Kansas border called Big Timbers. From a distance, what first appeared to be a blue hill proved to be a magnificent grove of ancient cottonwood trees, their leaves shimmering in the bright sunlight.

Andre told me that the grove, sometimes called Blue Mound, is a sacred place to the Indians. Their dead are often buried there. The Indians place them on scaffolds with all the objects they shall need for their new home. Perhaps placing a loved one close to the sky helps the Indian spirit leave the earth behind. The ceremony that takes place when an Indian dies suggests that Indians believe in an afterlife, as I do. When I heard this, I realized the white man and the Indian are equal in the last analysis.

The cool shade of the cottonwoods proved to be a great temptation after the heat we had endured. We put Old Granger and Mulberry out to graze. Then for a brief time, Andre and I walked together under the trees. The grass beneath our feet was adorned with clumps of bluebells.

Along the edge of the grove where the sun was constant, we smelled the pleasing aroma of Arkansas roses growing among an abundance of milkweed. Andre reached down and picked an erect, bright red bloom with tubular flowers and handed it to me. A milky substance exuded from its stem. He informed me it was a cardinal flower and had magical powers, being a very effective Pawnee love charm.

I took the flower without comment. What could I say? I could feel the charm working! So could Andre, by the look of him when my hand touched his.

Andre asked me unending questions about myself and my family. I answered him truthfully, but I neglected to mention the gold when I told him Father was a prospector. I let him think that Father, like so many others, had found the search for gold to be like chasing a will-o'-the-wisp.

I am very drawn to Andre, but I wonder about him. He wants to know everything about me, yet my inquiries of him are given an evasive answer.

After an hour's respite, we returned to the trail. We arrived at Goose Creek Station at dusk and made a cold camp.

Chapter Thirteen

Fort Wallace

July 7, 1867

WE REACHED FORT WALLACE without incident after three long days on the trail. We found water and grass in abundance at every stop along the way.

Early yesterday morning we headed for Willow Creek Station and arrived there late in the afternoon. Someone had named a patch of tall grass growing in a draw "Fitche's Meadow." The hay, which was excellent, can easily be cut and bundled for forage on the trail. We did not linger, but let the oxen drink their fill from a small stream and continued on our way. That night we camped on the prairie beside a spring.

Today, before we reached Fort Wallace, we passed Pond Creek Station where the railroad engineers had been accosted by Indians. I wondered if they were recovering from their wounds. It was an unfortunate turn of events for them, as they were only three miles from the safety of the Fort.

Fort Wallace is situated at the junction of Pond Creek and the south fork of the Smoky Hill River. The Fort, for the most part, consists of numerous tents and mule and horse corrals. The corrals are located haphazardly, and the Indians frequently drive off the Cavalry livestock with little consequence to themselves or their mounts. I shall take care that Old Granger and Mulberry are never placed in harm's way.

Lieutenant Hale of the 37th Infantry, the Fort's Commanding Officer, ordered Andre to locate a tent for us. Our residence at the Fort is a concession of Lieutenant Hale. Under normal circumstances we would not be allowed to remain here, but for him to send us elsewhere would endanger us. An Indian attack is always possible. The Fort is officially under siege. We pitched our tent away from Fort activity but close enough to afford us protection.

Fort Wallace is a bustling three-company Post of over two hundred men. There is construction everywhere, and five new stone buildings are almost completed. As of now, simple tents comprise most of the temporary quarters, including the Post hospital.

The hospital is a grim reminder of the mission of the men and women who live here. Doctor Bell, the Post physician, is charged with photographing the pitiful remains of the dead soldiers for the military's record before they are buried with the Honors of War.

In my opinion, it is wrong, except under extreme circumstances, to send small detachments of men out on patrol

Chapter Thirteen — Fort Wallace

where they are vulnerable. The Sioux and the Cheyenne often have as many as six hundred warriors in a single raiding party. I tremble inwardly, thinking my Andre might suffer the same fate as so many others. I call him "my Andre," but I cannot imagine it shall ever come to pass.

The hostiles have cut the telegraph wires all along the trail. The Fort has received no news, either from the east or the west, for several weeks. The stage from Denver City arrived carrying the wounded engineers, but traffic on the trail has been prohibited. We have been told not to expect to travel any time soon, though surprisingly, a bull train arrived here a week ago headed for Denver.

July 8, 1867

Today, just before sunup, the men in Camp Nineteen struck tents. Lieutenant Hale had organized a military escort of forty men for a party of one hundred-sixty railroad workers who were headed west. The railroad plans to survey for track that shall be built through Raton Pass in Colorado Territory. Restrictions on use of the trail evidently do not apply to the comings and goings of the men working on the railroad.

There was good news! The men who were wounded at Pond Creek shall recover from their injuries. They had quite a vigorous engagement against the twenty Cheyenne and were fortunate their scalps were not taken and used to decorate a Cheyenne war shield. It was for the best that Father and I were not on the stage when it was attacked. Father's weakened condition would have hampered the men.

Andre was not among the men ordered to protect the railroad crews. He visited our tent this morning to inform us he

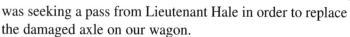

was seeking a pass from Lieutenant Hale in order to replace the damaged axle on our wagon.

If only I could determine whether or not Andre has discovered the hidden compartment. Nothing in his demeanor suggests he is aware of the gold. I find this to be a burden that needs resolution.

There was a flurry of excitement at the Fort today. A report came in that railroad crews laying a line of track eight miles west of Rose Creek had come upon an abandoned wagon and the bodies of two men. No one knows how the men died. They had not been killed by Indians. Instead, they appeared to have died either of foul play or hardships of the trail.

They found one man inside the wagon. He was folded in a blanket; an empty bottle of laudanum lay nearby. The other man was lying on the ground outside the wagon. He had been shot to death with the gun that lay beside him. The wagon contents offered no evidence of food, forage, or ammunition which would have suggested they might have been robbed, although why a gun was left behind seems strange. Two mules were still in their harnesses. They had been abused, and although half-starved, they were still alive. The soldiers unhitched them and turned them out to fend for themselves.

The two bodies were brought back to the Fort for identification. The description of the men so closely resembled Anton Dumler and Jacques St. John that Father asked for permission to visit the lime-house. His request was granted.

It was as Father suspected. Mr. Dumler and his cohort were dead. (May they rest in peace.) I doubt we shall ever know the circumstances surrounding their deaths. I would never disparage the dead, but I know in my heart that Mr. Dumler and Mr. St. John followed us, hoping to rob Father of his gold. I trust Mr. Atkinson has found business

Chapter Thirteen — Fort Wallace

 elsewhere. He did not join his two friends in their ill-conceived venture.

July 9, 1867

I awoke early this morning. The same cool breeze that caressed the buffalo grass was stroking my face. I heard the call of a turtledove, and somewhere on the prairie a meadowlark was singing. The sky was robin's egg blue, and creamy clouds stretched across the heavens in long ridges. The horizon was a pale shade of pink, the exact color I would choose for a dress if I were going to a ball, which of course I am not!

I felt a sense of security, prompted by our residence at Fort Wallace. The constraint that always exists when under siege had dissipated. Tethered close by under my watchful eye were Old Granger and Mulberry, spared the company of Cavalry horses and mules in the crowded corrals. I watched the sunrise and dreamed of Andre. If only he and I might somehow find a way to spend our lives together. I insist upon my dreams, even though they seem impossible.

When Father joined me, we brewed our morning coffee.

Father's health improves with each passing day. I have found another snakebite remedy, an Indian cure for pain. This one, blacksamson, aids his comfort. The extract from the blacksamson wildflower, growing in abundance hereabouts, is an excellent medicine. Father drinks the extract in his water, and I dress the wound with it several times a day.

In this pleasant setting I have mustered the courage to ask Father a personal question. I have always wondered why he gave up a comfortable life in New Bordeaux to become a prospector, risking everything in the quest for wealth. I suggested to him that if he had not been fortunate, he would have gambled away everything he owned and received nothing in return.

Father pondered his answer for some time. He said he had no idea why he took that chance. Failure had not occurred to him. What he was to do with his life had always been revealed to him as he went about his daily work. He desired the chance to give purpose to his existence and had often felt his work was important.

I asked Father if finding the gold had satisfied his determination to be successful.

His answer surprised me. The gold was not foremost in his mind. He said he was only a man where success was concerned, for although he realized that he had at times fallen short of the mark, in his heart he knew the man he should be. Finding the gold had nothing to do with his personal fulfillment. In all probability, he told me, he would die and never know why the Almighty had directed his footsteps to the gold in Clear Creek Canyon. He said his heart was content, for he had done his best to advance whatever part of God's greater plan was laid out for him to accomplish.

July 10, 1867

Except for shortages of certain medicines and some of the more essential staples, it is not readily apparent that Fort Wallace is strained, though Indian activity has isolated us. However, I fear everyone on the garrison shall soon experience hardship.

Father and I still have small amounts of the supplies we purchased in Denver City. Fortunately, at times we have been able to live off the land. I have charged Andre with trading or giving away some of our flour and dried beef as

Chapter Thirteen — Fort Wallace

the need arises to the women on the Post who have small children.

To some extent, the problem of shortages is the way the Army stores its food. The provisions are placed upon the ground and covered with a flimsy piece of canvas. After such treatment, the food is often not fit to eat due to exposure to the elements.

Then there is the poor quality of the food they have purchased. Much of it was packaged during the Civil War. To buy such goods and pass them along as acceptable merchandise to be used by the military constitutes a misuse of funds by the government agencies in charge of such matters. No doubt the difference in price goes into their own pockets. Such cheats!

In spite of the Indian threat, Father is impatient to return to the trail. It has been a month since he was bitten by the rattlesnake, and he is well on the mend. As for me, I would linger here indefinitely to be close to Andre.

July 11, 1867

This morning Andre appeared at our tent in time for breakfast. I was overjoyed to hear he had acquired a two-day pass. At last there was time to repair our wagon. Andre suggested replacing the broken axle with the good one from the abandoned wagon near Rose Creek.

I was making Rhode Island johnnycakes. To the cornmeal I added a tiny amount of sugar, then enough boiling water to wet the corn thoroughly. While the meal was still hot and light I added cold milk, making a batter that would drop easily from a spoon onto the hot griddle to fry into thin small cakes after turning several times. As I fried the johnnycakes in beef drippings, I mulled over ways to allow the axle to be replaced without revealing the compartment hidden under the wagon bed. All my mental calculations could not suggest a plausible plan.

Andre also requested, and Lieutenant Hale granted him, an armed escort of ten men and a Corporal. In light of recent Indian activity, I questioned the wisdom of retrieving a used axle. I reminded him of the large number of Cheyenne and Sioux that sometimes comprise a raiding party. Even a small war party often carries repeating carbines.

Andre was unconcerned. Not all Indians have repeating carbines, he insisted, and those who do are untrained. He went on to say that not even the bravest Indian wants to be in the first assault group to attack twelve trained and experienced riflemen. If the worst should happen, he said to me, we would be in excellent hands. The Cavalry would surely come to our rescue.

I was not comforted.

Andre also said that once the axle was recovered and brought to the Fort, the armed escort would be dismissed. Father's gold would remain secure.

Andre laughed at my startled demeanor and informed me he had not failed to notice the enclosed space and had concluded that Father was carrying a load of gold.

At first, Andre would not allow me to accompany him to Rose Creek. But I would not be dissuaded. His fate would be my fate, if we were accosted by the Cheyenne or the Sioux. I rode in a haywagon with five of the cavalrymen. Pride and Bruno accompanied us and were off chasing jackrabbits at every opportunity.

We found the discarded wagon where we were told it would be, and as I looked at the decrepit conveyance, I thought what a strange twist of circumstance that none other than Mr. Dumler's wagon should enable us to continue our journey!

Chapter Thirteen — Fort Wallace

Recovering the axle, however, was not a simple task. Andre and the men raised the rear of the abandoned wagon, one side at a time, with a long pry. Then they placed piles of rocks, some of which we had brought with us, ahead of each rear wheel. When the props were finished, the wheels just cleared the ground. Andre used a spanner to remove the large threaded nut from the spindle on each wheel. Once the wheels were free, Andre pulled them off and laid them upon the ground. He also loosened the iron clamps that held the rear bolster. The rear axle came free, and two of the men lowered it to the ground. Once the coupling pole was unpinned and removed, they slid the axle free and threw it into the haywagon.

The mission was accomplished. Andre took the reins and drove us back to Fort Wallace. We did not visit, but Andre's eyes told me all I need to know. I am sure he loves me.

July 12, 1867

It was midday before Andre and I finished replacing the axle. With our work achieved, we had the afternoon to ourselves. Throwing caution to the winds, we decided it was a fine day for a picnic. We took my rifle, some dried apple pie, and cold johnnycake, for we intended to walk among the hackberry trees and river willows growing along the banks of the Smoky. It was dangerous for us to stroll so far from the Fort, but we were both of a mind that we must have time together. We have an uncertain future.

Once we were hidden in the trees where we would not be observed, I removed my hat. Then I let my chestnut hair down around my shoulders.

At first, Andre was shy. After a time he embraced and kissed me. Although loath to do so, I soon pushed him away.

He was contrite, and I forgave him his ardor. I was afraid of the future. No doubt Andre and I shall soon go our separate ways; it was a painful prospect.

We sat for several hours in the tall grass, conversing on every subject. Before it was time to return to the Fort, I knew Andre was my soul mate. I gave him my grandmother's locket as a love token, which moved him deeply.

Andre told me about himself and his family. It was not at all reasonable of Andre's father, but he had blamed Andre for his wife's death. She died when Andre was born; therefore, he never knew his mother. I told him about my mother's unselfish love. I assured him his mother would never harbour such thoughts of blame but, instead, would rejoice that her son lived.

Andre's father is well off financially and willingly educated all three of his sons. However, he is of the old school when it comes to inheritance. Everything he owns eventually shall go to Andre's oldest brother, Charles. Andre is expected to fend for himself.

When Andre was nineteen and Daniel his younger half-brother seventeen, they were both told by their father to go out into the world and make something of themselves. The edict was a vague charge, to say the least. There was no time to consider what would satisfy Andre or his father in that regard.

When the South sought to secede from the Union, it marked the beginning of the Civil War. Andre and Daniel became Privates in the Union Army, eventually serving under its youngest Brigadier General, George Armstrong Custer.

Andre was with Custer in 1863 at Gettysburg when Confederate General J. E. B. Stuart was overcome by Custer's unit and again at Appomattox, in 1865, when Union troops stopped General Robert E. Lee. It was Custer who received the gallant Southerner's flag of truce. Andre witnessed everything on that historic day.

But Andre does not like to talk about the war. Several of his closest companions and Daniel died in Georgia's Andersonville Prison. Only the grace of God kept Andre from the same fate. He did mention that on two occasions he pulled Custer from beneath his dead horse.

After the war, Andre drifted from place to place. He was at odds with the world and trying to forget all he had witnessed. He joined the Cavalry in the fall of 1866, saying to himself a soldier's life was the only career open to him. The Civil War had touched his conscience, and his prompt response to his country's plea for volunteers had precluded any chance he might have had to join the business community.

Andre has told me he is passed over time and time again when promotions are considered. He has tried to be worthy of a command, but even with all his education and capabilities, he is ignored. I can tell Andre is unhappy to be treated in this manner. He does not know the reason why, and no one has had the courtesy to enlighten him.

Another problem, which we share jointly, is the fact that a Private in the Cavalry is almost indigent, earning only thirteen dollars a month. If we should marry, it has been said that a Private's wife living on the Post is expected to do the enlisted men's laundry should the Fort be shy of laundresses. I can accept this, but Andre cannot. Inasmuch as Andre does not make enough money to support a wife and a family, we are thwarted in our desire to marry, if Andre remains in the Cavalry.

When I mentioned my share of the gold and my dowry, which shall be substantial, I could see humiliation in Andre's eyes. The thought of living off his wife's money did not appeal to him. Speaking for myself, I do not think a person with wealth and someone without assets should not consider marriage. Self-respect can be kept by hard work and by careful accounting of how the money is spent. I tried to convince Andre not to look upon the gold as an obstruction to our marriage. Perhaps he listened to me. Yet, I am certain Andre shall not permit me to be a laundress.

Fate must intervene.

Chapter Fourteen

Custer and the Seventh Cavalry

July 13, 1867

AT NOON TODAY the following men rode into Fort Wallace: Lieutenant Colonel George Armstrong Custer, four Delaware Indian scouts, "Medicine Bill" Comstock, Custer's brother Tom, and six troops of the Seventh Cavalry. With the exception of Custer, the men appeared to be exhausted. Their horses were weary, and man and beast alike needed respite from the grueling pace set by their leader.

Custer was upset to find the Fort under siege. He was counting on acquiring fresh horses and supplies before moving on. Fort Wallace begins the final leg of Custer's scouting expedition. The Seventh is currently engaged in a mission, requiring chastisement of the marauding Cheyenne and their Sioux allies. Custer is charged with driving them back to their reservations.

Custer had set forth from Fort Hays, some 150 miles east on June 1st, taking his troops north, headed for the Platte River in the new state of Nebraska. From there the trail led him down the Republican River and, after a sojourn into Colorado Territory, the troops made their way south to Fort Wallace. From here they shall follow the Smoky Hill Trail east. They have suffered six weeks of marching and have covered over seven hundred miles.

I asked Andre what Custer had accomplished.

He informed me Custer's troops were grumbling and were calling the assignment a failure. The Cheyenne and the Sioux were far too clever to allow Custer to punish them in such a manner. The Indians made it clear to the soldiers who were pursuing them that they did not wish to be reprimanded or placed on reservations far away from their traditional homes.

I expressed sympathy for the red man.

Andre would hear none of it. With Custer's arrival, came tales of the loss of Lieutenant Lyman S. Kidder and the eleven men in his command. It seemed the Commander of the Second Cavalry at Fort Sedgwick in Colorado Territory sent a young Lieutenant to find Custer. The Lieutenant was to present Custer with new orders from Lieutenant General Sherman. The Lieutenant followed the wrong trail, failed to find Custer, and, unfortunately, the Sioux and the Cheyenne happened upon him and his men and killed them. Custer and his troops came upon the tragic scene at Beaver Creek yesterday. All they could do was dig a common grave for the victims.

Although I understand why Andre feels as he does, I still

Chapter Fourteen — Custer and the Seventh Cavalry

deplore the useless shedding of blood. Someday it must come to pass that all who inhabit the earth shall put down their arms. Reason and love of peace shall overcome the violence that appears to be linked to man's nature.

July 14, 1867

This morning I was close enough to observe Custer as he took leave of the Post Headquarters. He is a tall, wiry man with long legs and pale blue eyes. He has medium length, curly blond hair and a drooping mustache below his long nose. A red scarf was tied under his chin.

From the look of him, I would never want Custer to be angry with me, for his visage resembled a monarch's. I have heard that, like a king-of-arms, he recognizes very little in the way of higher authority. He goes about his business in whatever manner suits his inclination.

One thing can be said for Custer. He does not ask his men to do anything he is not willing to do himself. In the Civil War, he invariably led the charge in battle. Andre told me about the time he pulled Custer from beneath his dead horse at the battle of Antietam. After the battle, Custer sent for Andre to thank him for saving his life. In those days Andre worshiped Custer and would have done, without question, anything Custer ordered him to do.

Father plans to ask Custer for an escort to the railroad when he moves his troops east. For Father's sake, I hope Custer grants the request.

As for me, I am in a state of melancholy. I want to remain here with Andre. However, the way things are at present, we have no future. Our situation appears to be hopeless.

Chapter Fifteen

The Trek to Fort Hays

Fort Hays, July 20, 1867

MY WORLD HAS turned around since last I wrote.

Six days ago, on July 15th, rumors were flying from all quarters at Fort Wallace. Custer was reported to have had harsh words with Lieutenant Hale. Custer demanded a plan to end what he called, "a deplorable situation." He decried the lack of food, medicines, and other vital staples needed to sustain the number of people dependent on the Fort. As superior officer, he took matters into his own hands and organized a detachment of the Seventh Cavalry. He planned to go after the medicines and food himself.

Chapter Fifteen — The Trek to Fort Hays

With this in mind, he ordered four commissioned officers, including his brother Tom, two ambulances, four mules, a supply wagon, and seventy-two men to ride forced-march the one hundred fifty miles east to Fort Hays. Custer planned to load provisions from Fort Hays' supplies and return at once to Fort Wallace.

That same day I overheard the conversation of two officers. They claimed Custer was in a state of severe agitation. Upon his arrival at Fort Wallace, Custer had expected, but did not receive, letters from his beautiful wife Elizabeth, whom he calls Libby. Custer had left Libby at Fort Hays in early June when he began his scouting expedition. On July 14th, the day after Custer arrived, a report from the east reached Fort Wallace; Custer then learned his wife had survived a flood when Big Creek overflowed its banks. However, when cholera broke out, the courier reported, Custer's wife had departed the Fort. The bearer of the bad news could not tell Custer where Libby was at that time, or even if she was still alive.

The officers said Custer stormed about his tent like a caged animal. They declared he appeared to be so worried he was almost out of his mind. A number of his men concluded from his actions that Elizabeth Custer was the entire reason for the planned, forced march, not the food and medicines. Only Custer knows the truth. Fort Wallace was somewhat strapped, but conditions were not intolerable.

At two o'clock that afternoon Andre appeared at our tent, unable to suppress his excitement. Andre had come upon Custer, and upon seeing his old comrade in arms, Custer had embraced Andre and commanded him to drive one of the military ambulances on the march to Fort Hays.

Custer also assigned to Andre the care of a large bundle. He did not explain its contents. Its transport was to be kept secret. The bundle was not well wrapped and Andre was tempted to open it. To his credit, however, he did not succumb to curiosity, though while undertaking repairs to the bundle, Andre determined it contained artifacts taken from Indian burial sites. Such objects are highly prized by collectors in the East. In my opinion, robbing the dead was not an honorable thing for Custer to do.

Upon learning of the impending march, Father went to Custer's tent and asked to join him when he moved his detachment east. To Father's chagrin, he was refused. Custer claimed he would be moving too rapidly to be responsible for civilians.

Custer's treatment of Father was wholly callous! Thwarted and not in good temper, Father returned to our tent. We would disregard the verdict, he declared, and be on our way. Custer, he said, could not stop us from using the trail!

Andre was able to calm Father and prepare a plan. He advised us to load our wagon and eat a hearty meal. He said we would not eat again, except sporadically, for several days. Our plan was to drive the wagon down to the Smoky Hill River south of the trail, wait until Custer and his men passed by, then fall in behind them. By arrangement, Andre's ambulance would be at the rear of Custer's column.

We now required mules. Andre untethered Old Granger and Mulberry and started to lead them away. My heart was breaking, for along the trail Old Granger had been the source of my strength. I ran after Andre and handed him a large gold nugget. I asked him to give it to the person to whom he traded Old Granger and Mulberry and urge the man to keep the oxen safe from Indians, for soon I would send a bullwhacker to buy them back for triple their worth. I said "Good-bye" to both animals and told Old Granger that ere long, I would send for him and his indolent partner.

Chapter Fifteen — The Trek to Fort Hays

When Andre returned, he had traded Old Granger and Mulberry to Doctor Bell's wife for a pair of fine mules named Molly and Red.

The bugle sounded, calling Andre to duty. Father and I ate our early supper and began loading the wagon. At four o'clock we drove down to the Smoky, heading south and east, looking for a hiding place off the trail to wait for Custer.

The day was sultry, the atmosphere giving rise to wavy images that distorted the horizon in a peculiar fashion. As Molly and Red worked to pull us through the underwood along the river, what had been a clear day began to grow dark. Clouds low in the southwest drifted higher in the sky and piled menacingly overhead. The growl of thunder accompanied by the threat of rain made me uneasy. I wondered how fast the Smoky might become a raging torrent, sweeping us and everything else in its path to oblivion. Lightning cut the sky, followed by a cold wind. The first pelts of rain hit our backs as we struggled along our way. Suddenly, the sky was like a waterfall. Within twenty minutes the Smoky was full and overflowing, forcing us to higher ground. Shortly thereafter, the rain decreased in intensity, ending as abruptly as it began. The sky cleared and the sun created a rainbow at its eastern edge.

By then we were hidden in a clump of sandbar willows about a mile from Fort Wallace. We had several hours to wait. It was difficult to keep Bruno and Pride from barking. I sang songs my mother had taught me, which seemed to please them and helped keep them quiet.

After the rain, the prairie smelled sweet with the scent of wildflowers. I felt as clean as the drenched grass, and my anger at Custer faded. After all, I reasoned, Custer is only a man.

Late in the afternoon, in the distance, Father and I spied Custer's detachment. The men and horses were in a long double column. When Andre's ambulance had passed, I urged Molly and Red onto the trail. I planned to keep the column of cavalrymen in sight, but not join them. Father lay in the back of the wagon with Bruno and Pride, for his leg was still swollen.

Custer was, indeed, moving rapidly! It was difficult for me to keep the United States flag and Custer's personal guidon in my view. There were times when the column was so strung out that it was obvious the men who had been ordered to ride with Custer were exhausted, as were their horses. How Custer could remain undaunted by any extreme puzzled me. Molly and Red had been fed well and were rested, or I never could have kept them at Custer's pace.

Custer continued to march even after dark. One or two times during the night, Father and I observed small groups of cavalrymen suddenly pull away from the column. They would disappear into the darkness to hide in a clump of trees or a draw. The men were deserters, and I could not find it in me to blame them.

Andre was usually within my sight, although at times he pulled his ambulance ahead to stay with the detachment. If we lagged behind, I always made haste, urging Molly and Red along.

Late on the afternoon of the sixteenth, at half past eight, we arrived at Monument Station. Finally, Custer permitted his men to take a short break. They drank a quick cup of coffee, although no one was allowed to do more than stand beside his mount. I pulled our wagon behind a hillock and waited until Custer moved on. He did not see us, for he was intent upon his mission.

Two miles farther east, about nine o'clock, we came upon Monument Rocks, huge monoliths that thrust upward from

Chapter Fifteen — The Trek to Fort Hays

the level plain, their tall peaks and arches carved by the wind and rain.

It was here that Custer came upon Captain Frederick Benteen and a supply train headed for Fort Wallace. Later, I learned from Andre that Custer had helped himself to some of Benteen's supplies. Andre mentioned that Captain Benteen harbours a dislike for Custer. I am sure taking supplies intended for Fort Wallace did not endear Custer to the Captain.

While Custer and Captain Benteen attended to their business, Father and I hid among the trees on the riverbank. When Custer and the Captain each went on his way, we resumed our place behind the column of men and horses.

At Castle Rock, Custer met two mail coaches headed west. Although he did not have the authority to do so, Custer halted the coaches and searched the mail that they carried for letters from his wife. According to Andre there were none, and in all probability this increased Custer's anxiety for his wife's safety.

By noon on the seventeenth, Custer was four miles west of Downer's Station. Here the terrain was rough and strewn with small boulders, bedrock being only inches under the buffalo grass. The declining trail wended its way southeast, a distance away, but parallel to a chalk ridge, stretching the length of a long, serpentine ravine. The ravine was to our south. In the bottom of the ravine, hidden between its banks, flowed the Smoky Hill River. To our north was a flat, treeless plain.

Suddenly, one of Andre's mules threw a shoe. The mishap caused Andre to split from the column, which continued on down the slope. Andre pulled off the trail and waited for our wagon.

He had just finished pulling the nails from the mule's hoof and had removed the loose shoe, when some Cheyenne horses rode into view on the far side of the ravine. The sight caused me to feel faint. We could see Custer, still moving rapidly, about a half mile ahead of us. Andre picked up his carbine and fired five rapid shots into the air. The last six cavalrymen in the departing column looked back. Five of them pulled their horses around and galloped back along the trail, reaching us quickly. But our hopes for more assistance were crushed, for Custer continued on his way.

The ensuing battle was brief. We had no time to consider what would be our best defensive position. We had only enough time to collect our guns and effect a barricade using the ambulance and our wagon when the Cheyenne surrounded us.

The Cheyenne were dressed in war paint, with one Indian wearing a buffalo headpiece; all were armed for battle. Even the Indian horses were resplendent with lightning stripes painted down their forelegs. Most of the horses also had paint-circled eyes, or red or white hand prints on their flanks.

Finally, the sixth cavalryman came to our aid and arrived at the same time as the Cheyenne. Our latest ally had struggled with his conscience, and upon resolving to do the right thing, he came galloping toward us. To our dismay, his horse was shot from under him only yards away from our barricade. As luck would have it, he was pinned under the unfortunate animal.

Andre dropped his rifle and ran to his fellow soldier's aid. I must admit, fear rendered me unable to move. Andre pulled the soldier from under his dead horse as he had done for others many times in Civil War battles. The two men ran toward us, trying to reach the barricade before they might be killed. The rescued man arrived safely, still holding his carbine, which he leveled at a Cheyenne. But Andre was not as lucky as his comrade. An arrow pierced his left foot,

Chapter Fifteen — The Trek to Fort Hays

sending him sprawling. The Indian who had shot the arrow then turned his pony, lifted a tomahawk over his head, and galloped back toward Andre.

Fear gave me tremendous strength. I raised Father's buffalo gun, and as I fired, I ordered Bruno to attack the Cheyenne pony. The recoil of the gun rammed my shoulder, causing me to fall, though from the corner of my eye I saw Bruno leap over the wagon tongue, dash across the grass, and engage the pony by its nose. The fierce attack twisted Bruno's body, swinging him in midair. The galloping pony stumbled and was dragged to the ground. As a consequence, the Indian fell from his mount and hit the stony earth where he lay still.

As the Indian fell, coming to our rescue from the east we could see many Cavalry horses with riders bent low. The Cheyenne also saw the men and horses, and thinking that they were outnumbered, the war party fled the scene of the battle.

My shot had missed its mark, for the Remington certainly would have torn the Indian apart. He died by another means, and I am relieved that his blood is not on my conscience.

Meanwhile, amidst this fearsome turmoil, Bruno came at my call and received praise and approval for his courageous act. Father had placed a restraining hand on Pride's head, awaiting the outcome of the attack. Bruno had not required Pride's assistance.

The Indian pony was bleeding from its nose. The unfortunate beast struggled to its feet and galloped away, a hapless victim.

But dear Andre — an arrow was protruding from his foot and he had fainted from pain. Father broke off the feathered end of the shaft, then cut off Andre's boot and pushed the arrow on through the flesh and bone before Andre regained consciousness. One of the men had a flask of whiskey, which Father poured over the wound and bound it with a rag.

The cavalrymen with horses rode out in pursuit of the Cheyenne. However, they returned almost at once with one horse carrying two troopers on his back. The men who had come to our aid then refused to return to Custer's command. Instead, they headed north, leaving a mortally wounded horse in the ravine. The man whom Andre rescued cursed his luck and with hopeless resignation said it was only a matter of time before he would follow suit.

We hurried back to the trail, lest the Cheyenne should return for their dead comrade and take our scalps in the bargain.

I drove the ambulance carrying Andre. The soldier took the reins of our wagon. We whipped the mules into as fast a pace as the rocky trail would permit and all but flew across the ground. Down the trail our eyes met a sight that astonished us all.

Everywhere was evidence of a battle, for it was plain to see that many horses had churned and flattened the grass all around us. I saw a lance protruding from the ground, and not far off the trail, wearing a bridle and a saddle, was a lone Cavalry horse grazing in the short prairie grass. Upon seeing our wagon and the ambulance, the horse looked up. Suddenly, he tossed his head and, flipping the reins to one side, he broke into a gallop, soon disappearing far ahead of us down the trail. We slowed our mules to a walk and searched the landscape with our eyes for signs of life. Finding none, we hurried on our way.

Fifteen minutes later we reached Downer's Station. Custer was awaiting our arrival. The Cavalry horses were still in a double column ready to move out, and the men were drinking coffee and eating hardtack. It crossed my

Chapter Fifteen — The Trek to Fort Hays

mind to wonder if Custer would have stopped to rest if he had not had to deal with a skirmish.

Custer came to meet us; he was still astride his horse. His greeting was terse and unfriendly, rebuking Father for disobeying his orders.

I knew that Custer had finally met his match.

"I am Pierre Prideaux," Father informed him, in no uncertain terms. "I am under no obligation to follow orders from the military!" Father declared that as this was a free country, he would go where he pleased, any time it suited him.

Custer's face resembled carved stone. His eyes glittered angrily, but he made no reply.

Our main concern was Andre. Father asked Custer what provisions would be made for him. Andre was now conscious; his face was etched with pain.

Custer had the decency to ride his horse to the back of the ambulance and speak to Andre. When Custer returned, he informed us he had made arrangements for Andre to remain at Downer's Station, in the company of Private James Gilcrest, who — oddly enough — had also been wounded through the foot by the Cheyenne when several troopers had lagged behind Custer's column and had been cut off by a band of hostiles! One man was killed. Luckily, Trooper Gilcrest had made his way back to Custer's command.

Andre and Private Gilcrest were placed in the care of the two stationmasters, where they were to remain until they recovered sufficiently to be taken to Fort Hays. I did not want to leave Andre, but both he and Father insisted upon it.

Andre's ambulance and the bundle of artifacts were placed in the care of a different driver. We were told to remain with Custer. When we were informed that the dead cavalryman was still at the site of the battle, we asked Custer to retrieve the man's body. He ignored our request.

Close to dawn on July 18th, we arrived at Big Creek Station south of Fort Hays. Custer requested a Captain Hamilton and others to escort us to the Fort. He obviously had no plans to go there himself.

Captain Hamilton was friendly, and as he had experienced his own trials with Custer, he understood our frustration. Father said Custer would be called to task for his behavior during the past several days. He cited Custer's refusal to pursue the Cheyenne who attacked us as well as his own men, and worst of all, his refusal to send men to recover the body of the cavalryman who was killed. I asked Captain Hamilton to tell me the name of the dead man. He was Private Harvey of H. Troop. I pray his family never learns how callously he was treated.

I find it difficult to reconcile the brave and brilliant Custer whom Andre knew and loved during the Civil War with the driven man we so briefly encountered. But judgment must come from another quarter. Only God is qualified to decide Custer's merits.

Chapter Sixteen

Gold Returned to Home

Late Evening, July 20, 1867

WHEN WE REACHED Fort Hays late morning on the 18th, we were exhausted. We pulled our wagon behind a stone wall, intending to contact the Fort's Commanding Officer later that day. After watering Molly and Red in Big Creek, we tethered them nearby. Then we ate a light meal and slept, undisturbed by the comings and goings of those around us.

At dusk I awoke and found Father ill in his bed. He was feverish and was suffering severe abdominal cramps. What food he had eaten, he had regurgitated.

The Post hospital proved to be merely a large tent staked to the ground on a rise south of Big Creek. I described Father's symptoms to the hospital steward. He in turn consulted Dr. Lippincott, the Post surgeon.

While awaiting their verdict, I cast furtive glances around the ward. The patients were not all men. Several women and two children were lying on the narrow cots within the tent. All appeared to have the same severe symptoms as Father. Fear gripped me. I realized I was witnessing the onset of an epidemic.

When the steward returned, he was the bearer of ominous tidings. Father had cholera. Its cause was unknown. There was no cure.

Father was brought to the hospital to lie with the other victims of the dread disease. Kindly hands nursed him. The Sisters of Mercy, a Catholic order, had offered their services to the Post during the crisis. The hospital staff welcomed my willingness to stay and lend aid.

The disease quickly becomes fatal, and it was soon apparent that Father was dying. It was two hours before midnight when he becn'd to me. I hurried to his bedside and listened to his whispered words. He spoke of his love for my mother and for me, and also his respect for Andre. Then he voiced one last request.

It was not easy to comply with his wishes. I waited a short while until the hospital staff was occupied with the latest cholera victim, one of the nuns, before I attempted the task. When no one was observing us, I helped Father up from his bed and supported him as he painfully made his way out of the tent. The hot night wind moaned, seemingly cognizant of the human tragedy unfolding as we walked slowly toward our wagon and the mules. When Father collapsed near the wagon, our mule Red who was tethered nearby served as a crutch. If we were missed at the hospital, no one came to find us. Perhaps they surmised Father preferred to die alone.

The time just before midnight was devoted to Father's gold. After setting aside my own and a generous amount in Pikes Peak coin for my dowry, as well as Father's gift to Andre, I buried the remainder. Women have always been vulnerable in a man's world. Father reasoned I might be robbed. If someone should steal my gold, Father's share was in a place where I could find it.

When we had finished our secret task, Father was too weak to walk back to the hospital. He died in my arms soon after I had buried the gold.

Before the sun came up the military arrived with a wagon and gathered up the civilian dead for burial. I had neither the skill, wood, nor time to make a coffin, so Father was placed in a folded sheet of canvas like all the others who had passed away during the night. I laid a crucifix in his hands and said a prayer before they left with him and the others. They took them across Big Creek to a graveyard used by the Hays City townspeople atop a hill. Pride followed the body of his master as far as the bridge on the Fort road. His mournful howl lingered in the gray dawn.

Father's dreams and his golden cache now sleep as he does, under the clay and loam of Kansas, back to the earth from whence they came, perhaps forever.

Chapter Seventeen

Yvette's Riddle

November 20, 1867

THE PAST FOUR months have flown by! August and September were behind Andre and me before we realized the changing of the season. October's brisk, sunny days and vivid blue skies disappeared. November's short, somber days mark time. Winter shall bring blizzards to the Plains. So much has changed!

Since Father died, I have experienced both deep grief and great joy. I now know I can face adversity and persevere. The memory of my parents, in whose home I always felt a great sense of belonging, shall never be

Chapter Seventeen — Yvette's Riddle

more than a thought away. Time has mellowed my unhappiness, and today I joyfully face the future as Mrs. Andre Lesseps.

As I pen the final entry in my journal, my husband Andre and I are seated on a bench near the train terminal in Junction City, a town close to Fort Riley that is one hundred-sixty miles from Fort Hays. We are on our way home to New Bordeaux. Pride and Bruno are with us, traveling with Molly and Red in a private boxcar. I have sent for Old Granger and Mulberry, who are doing well I am told. When they arrive in New Bordeaux, from that day they shall be free of a yoke around their necks.

I have purchased a two-hundred-acre farm near my childhood home. The farm shall be my responsibility. Andre has chosen to establish himself in the brickmaking business, of which he has some knowledge. In his wanderings after the Civil War, he resided at the home of a brickmaker and his son who worked at the trade. Andre has sent a letter to the younger man, offering him a lucrative position as manager of the kilns. Andre shall see to the needs of the customers.

Contentment fills my heart as I listen to the barking cries of a skein of snow geese flying high overhead. Perhaps they foretell a happy and secure future for Andre and me, for the snow geese never fail to have faith in the seasons. They prompt me to be grateful for my new life and the peace I have found. It is a welcome respite from the uncertainty of the past.

While Andre and I sit under a small white elm tree waiting to board the train, I reflect upon the future of our country. If Andre and I live long enough, we are certain to witness the end of the Indian Wars. When the white man and the red man resolve their differences and live together in peace, I shall thank God. I would like to see my country a hundred years hence. Perhaps by then our leaders shall have learned to solve difficult problems without bloodshed.

My journal would be incomplete if I did not relate the events occurring after Father's death. With this in mind, I refer back in time to July 19th, the morning of the day that Father died.

It was past dawn, Father's body had been carried away, and I remember the moments betwixt fitful sleep and waking. When I opened my eyes, the sun was shining, making it a beautiful day. As I recalled the events of the past night, I tried without success to quell my tears, only at last forcing myself to see to the needs of the animals.

I untethered Molly and Red and led them down the slope past the mule corral to Big Creek. It was in my thoughts to also bring back a bucket of water in which to bathe. I had neglected my toilet for some time. As Molly and Red quenched their thirst, I noticed the Cavalry mules and horses were also drinking from the creek. Their corral provided them access. The excrement from the corral could not help but sully the water, so I decided not to bathe. I was astonished to see a woman dip a bucket from the creek to use for drinking water.

Bruno and Pride were hungry, but food did not appeal to me. I drank a cup of hot coffee and forced myself to eat dried fruit and a piece of cornbread, for I am much too thin. As I struggled to swallow my food, I assessed my situation. By the time I had finished my meal, I had devised a plan.

I resolved, first of all, before attending to my own needs, to make secure what was left of Father's gold. I rolled stacks of gold coins, pouches of gold dust, and many large nuggets in several layers of cloth. When I was finished, I tucked the

Chapter Seventeen — Yvette's Riddle

rolls neatly into four leather bags, filling them completely. I saved back a generous amount of coin for my current needs. After disposing of the poisoned sugar, I placed the coins in the leather pouch hanging from my waist.

The gold was not yet secure. I soaked buffalo-tug thongs in water, and when they were thoroughly saturated, I bound each bag. The wet leather dried in the heat of the sun, shrinking the strands until they were like iron bands. No one could ascertain the bags' contents unless he deliberately cut the thongs. Their weight was considerable, but I lifted them into the back of my wagon.

I drove to the tent that served as Post Headquarters and asked to speak to the Commanding Officer. This proved to be Major Alfred Gibbs of the Seventh Cavalry, a perceptive man wearing a mustache and a goatee. The Major was a West Point graduate and a veteran of the Mexican War, the Civil War, and numerous Indian campaigns. Although Major Gibbs was strict with his men, he could not have been more courteous to me. When I confessed to the Major that I was a girl masquerading as a boy, he was most solicitous and sent for his wife. Major Gibbs' wife proved to be a charming and practical woman who constantly fussed over her husband, for Major Gibbs suffered unrelenting pain caused by old battle wounds.

At Major and Mrs. Gibbs' suggestion, I delivered my leather bags to the Sutler's store for safekeeping in the Post commissary safe. I told the Major the bags contained items of value given to me by my father. My explanation was close enough to the truth. The Major did not question me further.

Once the gold was safe, I accompanied Mrs. Gibbs to her home which was a recently built, two-family dwelling on Officers Row. One apartment was the Gibbs' quarters. Mrs. Gibbs explained Fort protocol to me. Unless I was the guest of an officer's family, I would be forced to live in town. But she did not consider Hays City to be a safe place, especially for young ladies, and I was, therefore, invited to stay with them. I was most grateful for their generous hospitality.

But poor Molly and Red were not permitted to remain on the Post. They were sent across Big Creek to the livery stable. This was after the military had placed my wagon in storage behind a blacksmith shop, just east of the Fort road.

Bruno and Pride presented a small problem as well. Mrs. Gibbs did not want them in her fine house. Of course, I understood her reasons. My faithful companions were forced to content themselves with languishing upon the front porch. They kept company, not only with other dogs, but with a variety of domesticated wildlife, raccoons, opossums, and squirrels.

When I mentioned Andre and expressed my concern for his welfare, Mrs. Gibbs assured me she would inquire after him.

Because I was disreputable in my attire, I devoted a portion of my time to bathing and donning clean clothes. There was a rain barrel at the corner of the porch, and I was given permission to use the water. Mrs. Gibbs sent me to the back room of the kitchen where there was a small copper bathtub and bars of Castile soap. At the same time she offered me a choice of several of her own dresses. I chose a pale pink gingham with a plain high collar. It did not fit properly, as it was somewhat large for me, but I tied it in at the waist with a white sash.

My cowhide boots were a source of embarrassment to me. I had seen only one woman wearing boots. Mrs. Gibbs offered to take them to a bootblack, hoping to improve their appearance. In the meantime, she explained to me that women do not wear their unbound tresses in public. She

Chapter Seventeen — Yvette's Riddle

combed my hair for me and tucked it into a crocheted snood, one that had been made quite attractive with elaborate beadwork.

For an entire day, I sat in the kitchen drinking hot tea and visiting with Mrs. Gibbs and the other ladies on the Post. Until then I had not realized the extent to which I had missed the company of my own gender.

We talked at length of the stranding of the steamship *Santiago de Cuba* last June on Absecom Beach near Atlantic City, New Jersey. The niece of one of the ladies had been in the third boat to leave the ship. The seas had run high and the lifeboat was capsized, drowning the lady's niece and three other women as well as one child and a seaman. I was not the only person sitting at the table who had recently lost a loved one.

Someone mentioned the nun who had become ill with cholera and had died the same night that Father had succumbed. I realized I was derelict in my duty by ignoring the sick while sitting at Mrs. Gibbs' fine table. I said farewell to the ladies and presented myself at the hospital tent. For two days I did my best to help alleviate the suffering of the victims of cholera.

Early on the morning of my third day at the hospital, a courier from Major Gibbs' office came to see Dr. Lippincott. The man informed us that a message from Downer's Station had arrived requesting the services of a surgeon. It had been almost a week since Andre was wounded, and his foot had not responded well to the ministering of the stationmasters. They sent word that Andre would not live unless his leg was removed from the knee down.

I was filled with fear! I knew Andre would never willingly let the surgeon cut off his leg. I hurried to Major Gibbs' tent. He was in his office seated at his desk. I asked him for an escort to Downer's Station that I might nurse

Andre. When he declined to provide one, I opened my leather pouch, poured the gold it contained onto his desk, and fell to my knees, begging him to reconsider.

Major Gibbs stared at the gold in stunned silence. He rose from his seat, gathered up the coins and helped me to my feet. He put the gold back in my hands, saying a payment was not necessary. Words cannot express my gratitude for his generosity. A Lieutenant, ten men, and an ambulance were summoned, and that same day I was taken to Andre.

Before I left Fort Hays, I went to the hospital tent and asked Dr. Lippincott if he intended to come with me. He was understandably preoccupied. His wife had contracted cholera, and she had just recently been brought to the hospital. He was intent upon treating her symptoms, trying to keep enough fluids in her body to sustain her life. He promised me he would come to Downer's Station as soon as he could, and he instructed a nun to give me the medicines and bandages I would need to treat Andre.

I availed myself of the following supplies: carbolic acid, muslin bandages, a needle, oiled thread, a bar of Castile hand soap, alcohol, whiskey, bromine, chloroform, opium pills, and a vial of paregoric. As an afterthought, I went to the sutler's store and purchased extra ammunition, candles, tea, rice, dried beef, a jug of molasses, and five pounds of salt.

I was prepared for any contingency when I climbed into the ambulance. Bruno and Pride joined me, one on either side of the conveyance. It was a forty-mile trip to Downer's Station. We arrived there well after dark.

Andre's bed was in a tiny, dimly lit room on the second floor of the building. It was sweltering under the tin roof. Even with two small windows open, there was no breeze. He tried unsuccessfully to sit up when I entered the room, and I cried when I saw him, for he lacked a healthy

Chapter Seventeen — Yvette's Riddle

complexion. He seemed almost like a child in need of his mother. I put my arms around him and said I would not leave him. He was not to worry. All would be well.

Our reunion was cut short by the officer in charge. He marched up the stairs and intruded upon us. Of course, this was his right, for Andre was in the military. The officer asked to see Andre's foot, saying he would take back a report to his superior officer. Andre's foot was covered with a white cloth, which the officer set aside.

The bandage applied by Father six days ago had been removed by one of the stationmasters. The wound was open to the air, and I was thankful that it did not appear to be gangrenous. I would not need the chloroform and bromide. Instead of dead and dying body tissue, the foot was red and swollen. Ugly red streaks ran up the length of Andre's leg, almost to his knee. The officer asked Andre if he had feeling in his foot. It was a small comfort to have him answer in the affirmative.

One of the stationmasters was hovering nearby. He maintained Andre suffered from poisoned blood and would surely die if his leg did not come off.

Andre said he would rather die than lose his leg.

The officer was in a quandary. He turned to me and asked if I was a nurse.

I looked again at the red streaks on Andre's leg. The streaks reminded me of the time when I was a child and the wind slammed the cabin door shut on my finger. Mother had gently washed my crushed finger in soapsuds and wrapped it in a bandage. Several days later I had red streaks on my arm up to my elbow.

Father had lifted Mother's wooden wash tub down from its peg on the wall and filled the tub with warm water. He added salt crystals to the water, making a brine. I frequently soaked my hand and arm in the warm brine for many days until the red streaks disappeared. My parents took turns, day and night, keeping the water in the tub a constant temperature with hot stones from the fire. I knew I could use the same treatment for Andre's leg.

I told the officer to come back with Dr. Lippincott in seven days. If Andre's foot was not better by then, Andre would have to choose between living as a cripple or dying.

Within an hour after immersing Andre's foot in the warm brine, the heat was working its curative powers, and by midnight Andre had fallen asleep. One of the stationmasters said it was the first time the pain in Andre's foot had alleviated enough to allow him restful slumber.

By the first day of August, the swelling in Andre's foot was much reduced. Dr. Lippincott was told his services were not needed. Andre's improvement was remarkable, and the stationmasters teased me and told me I was a good nurse. The older man remarked that if a Cheyenne ever got him he would straightaway send for me! He was glad he had been wrong about Andre's leg.

I laughed and told both stationmasters to stay alert if the Cheyenne appear, for I had no desire to be in charge of a hospital!

Also, it was with pleasure that I learned of Private James Gilchrest — he was doing well, though he most likely shall not be suited for a life in the Cavalry due to the extent of his injury.

The months of September and October were filled with happiness for Andre and me. That we loved each other was obvious to the stationmasters. It is to their credit they found chores to occupy themselves, leaving us to idle away the hours as lovers always do. Mercifully, the Cheyenne did not attack Downer's Station during the time Andre was ill.

While Andre's foot was healing, we often applied horse liniment to the injury. We worked the liquid into the bones

Chapter Seventeen — Yvette's Riddle

and muscles, trying to make Andre's foot usable again. He could not walk at all for the first four months of his recovery, but as of now he walks with the aid of two canes. I believe someday he shall be able to put them aside.

In early November the Post's surgeon, Dr. Mecham, rode to Downer's Station to examine Andre. Dr. Lippincott's wife had died, and he was no longer at the Fort. I was sorry to hear the sad news.

Upon completion of Andre's examination, Dr. Mecham gave Andre a Surgeon's Certificate, confirming the fact that Andre also could no longer perform his duties in the Cavalry. After that, a letter came from Major Gibbs telling Andre that the Cavalry regretted losing him, but the injury he had sustained was far too disabling to permit him to remain.

Andre has no pension. I now thank God I spent many back-breaking hours gleaning gold from Clear Creek with Father.

Andre continued to improve, but before we could think of traveling to Missouri, three obligations needed tending. First, of course, was our marriage. We asked the Post Chaplin, Captain Charles Cole, to perform the ceremony, which took place in Major and Mrs. Gibbs' parlor. We shall be married again in New Bordeaux by a priest, but only to provide a satisfactory answer to my relatives' probing questions.

I shall treasure the memory of my wedding day as long as I live. I wore one of Elizabeth Custer's white muslin dresses. Because I am taller than Mrs. Custer, Mrs. Gibbs added lace to the sleeves and hem. I could find no flowers. Instead, I picked a bouquet of bittersweet and tied it to my prayer book with a white ribbon. Andre produced his mother's pearl ring. It was not a wedding band, but that was of no consequence. Mrs. Gibbs baked a wedding cake, and each officer's wife produced a memento from among her personal possessions. I can truthfully say, that day was the happiest I have ever known!

Our second commitment was to visit Father's grave. A military ambulance was put at our disposal by Major Gibbs. On the afternoon of the day Andre and I were married, we visited the civilian cemetery in Hays City. I was moved to tears when I saw the lonely graves, the sad mounds of gray clay and creeping runners of buffalo grass.

Cholera victims were not the only persons buried on the hill. The latest grave, according to a wooden marker, was that of a young man who died in a gunfight at Tommy Drum's Saloon.

Most of the graves were without headstones. Those with an identity had monuments made of Georgia marble or wood. Nothing told me which of the unmarked graves was my father's final resting place. But it occurred to me that it was unnecessary for me to find the site. I believe death was not the end for him. He did not ask to be born. He did not choose when to die. His soul still lives. I said a prayer and placed my bittersweet on one of the unmarked graves.

The third obligation concerned Father's gold. The day after my wedding, I walked alone to the place where the gold was buried. Not a trace of displaced soil remained to suggest what lay beneath the ground's surface. I had walked Red and Molly back and forth over the location, trampling the earth until my handiwork was completely obliterated.

I am tormented. Should I, or should I not, reveal the location of my father's buried gold? First, let me assure you of

Chapter Seventeen — Yvette's Riddle 139

 this absolute truth: Gold does not buy good health, peace of mind, or the sincerity of one's fellow man. Indeed, it often brings a generous measure of grief.

I have decided that if I am blessed with children, I shall tell them about their grandfather's buried treasure. I shall also give them my journal and a riddle that will hold the key to the location of the gold. Whoever solves the riddle shall find the gold.

> *Upon the Fourth a fortnight past,*
> *The fortress sleeps.*
> *The hands at five, due west.*
> *As heaven's light appears at dawn,*
> *Creeps downward, brings to notice*
> *Earth that welcomes gold returned to home.*

The train whistle is telling Andre and me to climb aboard. I must conclude my journal, for I am beginning a new season in my life. I shall not fail to remember my parents and all that was granted to me in my youth by a clement God. But as is the way of the world, the past has gone. I now anticipate the future, looking back in time only to reassure myself that Father would approve my stewardship of his gold.

Yvette Marie Prideaux Lesseps

July 14, 1967

Julia closed Yvette's journal and brushed her hand lightly across the worn cover. After a moment's silence, Chris rose from his chair and walked to the window. The warm breeze wafted through the room, carrying to his ears the indistinct sounds of the workday.

"That's quite a story. It tells a lot about Yvette's life; I feel like I know her. If I had lived back then, I think Andre would have had a little competition!"

"I could be Andre's soul mate for that matter," said Julia. "It's odd, how their personalities mesh with ours!"

Julia picked up her book bag, shoved the journal inside, and buckled the flap. "But the point is, we still have no idea where the gold is buried."

"We can't escape the fact that it all boils down to the riddle," said Chris. "The riddle holds the key to the location of the gold. Those were Yvette's exact words!"

"I've analyzed that riddle in every possible way," exclaimed Julia with frustration. "The riddle has never made sense to anyone. We're all missing something important!"

Chris closed the windows and took the key to the house from his pocket. Then he pulled Julia to her feet and kissed her.

Several minutes later Chris said, "Maybe we need to back off for a bit where the gold is concerned. We're trying too hard. There's still time left. Matt isn't due to arrive home for at least three weeks!"

Julia's hopes were at a new low. "I suppose the gold will stay hidden for another hundred years!"

Chapter Eighteen

How Perfectly Logical!

July 17-18, 1967

MONDAY WAS A routine day at Fort Hays. After work Chris and Julia swam at the municipal pool, then Chris went home to do his chores.

On Tuesday, July 18th, at nine o'clock in the morning, Julia asked Jennifer for permission to give the house on Officers Row a thorough dusting. Julia rummaged in the broom closet for cleaning supplies — a lambswool duster and mop, a dust rag, and a bottle of lemon oil — then stepped into Jennifer's office and picked up the key to the house. The day was warm, so before Julia left the Visitor's Information Center she took coins from her purse and bought a canned drink from the vending machine beside the front door.

Julia walked slowly across the parking lot to Officers Row. She was followed by Old Major who nudged her pocket in hopes of obtaining one of his treats. As Julia placed her cleaning supplies on the veranda and unlocked the front door, thoughts of Chris, the unsolved riddle, and Pierre Prideaux's lost gold were spinning in her mind.

Old Major insisted upon his treat, so Julia reached into her pocket and pulled out a dog biscuit, telling him, "You wait here."

Old Major accepted his treat and walked past his customary place under the window, then flopped down in the shade on the northwest side of the house.

Once inside, Julia closed and locked the door behind her. A cursory glance around the room told her it would take at least two hours to complete her task. She looked for the best place to begin her work.

The kitchen had a long pine table in the center of the room, and there were five large windows along the southeast wall. The early morning sun filled the room with light, and Julia decided to begin her work there, before the day became too hot. She lifted three of the window sashes to let in outside air. Because the morning sun was bright, she removed the tiebacks on the muslin curtains and let the fabric fall straight, blocking the sun's glare. Minute holes in the woven fabric created tiny flecks of light low on the northwest wall of the room.

She placed her cleaning supplies on a cast-iron cook stove, then opened the bottle of lemon oil and applied a dab to her dust rag. She popped the cap on her soft drink, took a sip, and set the can down in the dry sink. The soda fizzed as Julia took another cool swallow.

Between sips, Julia wiped her oiled rag alternately after the lambswool duster, across the surfaces of the room's tables. She stood on a chair to dust the kitchen shelves. Then, finally, she chased the dust bunnies from the corners of the room with her wool dust mop. When she glanced at her wristwatch, to her annoyance she found she had forgotten to put it on. However, she noted

Chapter Eighteen — How Perfectly Logical!

that the sun had climbed higher in the sky. The light rays on the wall had drifted sideways and down, closer to the floor.

Once the kitchen was dust free, from the edge of the veranda Julia shook her mop and duster. Then she focused her attention on the parlor. As she worked, she mused about Mrs. Gibbs, the long-dead officer's wife who had made a home for her husband, the Major, in the very house that Julia was cleaning.

"What was it like to live at Fort Hays a hundred years ago?" Julia spoke aloud, although no one was there to hear her.

Holding the dust rag, Julia's hands moved across the surface of the pump organ, then stopped. For a long moment, they rested quietly on the silent keys. A puzzled look was on Julia's face as she laid her rag on the organ's swivel seat and went into the kitchen to retrieve her soda. Several minutes passed as Julia stood next to the kitchen table, staring at the wall. By then the shafts of light had rearranged themselves in a pattern of bright dots on the kitchen floor.

Chills ran up and down Julia's spine, and she licked her lips as insight slowly dawned.

"Creeps *downward!*" she murmured, as if to the spirit of Mrs. Gibbs who had occupied the kitchen a century earlier. "How perfectly logical! It's the *only* place where Pierre could have buried his gold!"

Julia smiled to herself as she hurriedly finished her work, then gathered together her cleaning supplies. When she left the house, she locked the door and quickly called to Old Major. He rose from his nap and slowly followed along behind her.

Julia's heart was almost singing. She told herself she would likely have enough gold to buy Matt a horse ranch when he arrived home! And if Pierre's gold was not where she thought it was, she reasoned, it would be because it had been found by accident long ago, and a hundred years of her family's efforts to locate it would have been a waste of time.

Julia left the house on Officers Row to meet Chris for lunch beneath the elms near the parking lot. He was unaware that Julia had been working in the house. As she approached, he rose to his feet, instinctively knowing from her expression that something important had taken place.

"I *know* where Pierre buried his gold! No wonder it has never been found!"

Chapter Nineteen

Thanks to Old Major

After 5:30 PM, July 18, 1967

THE SECOND THAT Fort Hays closed its doors to the public on Tuesday evening, Julia and Chris were in Jennifer's office.

Jennifer turned to Julia. "The decision really isn't mine. Besides, your request is unprecedented. To be frank with you, I'm caught between my curiosity about the existence of the gold and my obligations as Fort Superintendent. The Fort is now an historic site. Digging by unauthorized persons is not permitted . . . though there may be a way around that.

"I think I've devised a way to look for the gold and still adhere to the Historical Society's regulations. In all probability, I'm stretching my authority . . . I hope you understand my position!

"Months ago, I sent a requisition to Topeka asking them to repair the blockhouse floor strictly from a safety point of view. At the time, funding was not available. Today I called the state office and was given the "go ahead" to hire a local contractor.

"Before he arrives, we will excavate the site. But you both must agree to sift the displaced soil, in an effort to locate small objects such as buttons, nails, pottery, or glass shards that might be discovered."

Julia glanced at Chris and he nodded.

"Then it's agreed!"

Jennifer took a set of keys from her desk and everyone left the center, locking it for the night. Once outside, they headed east toward the blockhouse. As they passed the maintenance tool shed, Chris entered the building and selected a pair of pliers, a crowbar, and a shovel. As an afterthought, he picked up two small tarpaulins.

Old Major was in the shed where he had just finished his supper. When he realized something was afoot, he circled around the trio, eagerly sniffing at the tools. Strangely, he knew where they were going and loped ahead, disappearing behind the northeast wing of the blockhouse. Jennifer, Julia, and Chris found him seated next to the east door. Jennifer unlocked the door, and everybody went inside.

Upon entering the room, Old Major walked across the floor to the west wall of the octagon-shaped building and sniffed along the baseboard.

Julia stared at Old Major and said to Chris, "What on earth is he doing?"

"Animals are aware of more than we think. I wish Old Major could talk."

After examining the baseboard, Old Major moved to the center of the room and flopped on the floor.

Jennifer pulled up two chairs, one for herself and one for Julia, then said, "Tell me again how you made this discovery."

As Chris began the task of prying up the wide pine planks to expose the earth that was directly under the floor, Julia explained

Chapter Nineteen — Thanks to Old Major

to Jennifer how she was able to ascertain the meaning of Yvette's riddle.

"Cleaning Mrs. Gibbs house on Officers Row caused me to imagine Fort Hays as it was when Yvette first arrived here. It was an uncanny feeling, pretending I was living in 1867, but in my mind's eye I could see everything on the garrison. Back then the Fort consisted mostly of tents and one or two wooden buildings. Officers Row had only one house. The limestone guardhouse didn't exist. This building, the blockhouse, was new, and was the only stone building on the Post. It was a defense barricade when Pierre and Yvette had arrived here.

"I could see the workmen as they built up the east wall. I saw them fitting the angle of the gunslits to maximize the safety of the riflemen using the openings. I saw the morning sun shining through the openings. The bright light made a pattern on the west wall which was *due west* because of the octagon shape of the building. And as the day wore on, the squares of light slowly drifted down the rock until they lay on the ground, on the place where the gold was buried. I remembered the blockhouse wasn't the Post Headquarters until later, when it was redesigned and the gun slits were sealed.

"Pierre probably drove his wagon inside the six-sided enclosure without permission. No one noticed him. He was hidden from view, unless someone happened to look through one of the entryways. Pierre had likely been told to drive his team across Big Creek into Hays and find a place to stay off the garrison, as civilians were only allowed on the Fort premises by invitation. But he and Yvette had reached a sanctuary, and he didn't want to leave.

"When Yvette awoke the morning after Pierre's death, the sun was shining through the gun slits. She sat inside the fortification grieving for her father and watching the pattern of light creep down the west wall until it reached the ground to the place where she had buried Pierre's gold. I have a feeling the gold is still here!"

As Chris pried up another floorboard, he looked up at Julia and Jennifer. "Yvette was lucky she didn't die with cholera, too. I wonder how she escaped."

The same question had occurred to Julia, but she had figured that out.

"Back then they didn't know cholera came from contaminated food and water. Yvette wouldn't bathe in the water from Big Creek. She probably avoided drinking it, too. She drank water from her own supply and she drank hot coffee and tea, which she made from boiled water. That's the only plausible explanation I can offer for her luck. As for Pierre, there's no telling where he picked up the disease. It can kill within twelve hours."

Excitedly, Julia reached down and laid aside the last floorboard, exposing the crosspieces of timber and the hard earth beneath them. Chris picked up his shovel, worked it into the dry dirt, and began to dig. Julia could not sit idly by and she picked up the soil with her hands and dumped it on one of the tarps. The smell of earth filled the room. There was not much space for Chris to maneuver between the floor joists, and his shovel cut down only seven or eight inches. But he persisted, and after considerable effort he managed to spade up the entire length of the west wall. A second digging, not as deep, yielded nothing. He was exhausted and a bit out of sorts when he turned to Julia and Jennifer.

"If this is where Pierre and Yvette hid the gold, it has already been found!"

Chris dropped his shovel on the pile of dirt and studied a blister on the palm of his hand. He had forgotten to bring along a pair of gloves.

Julia was on the verge of tears, but she was not willing to admit defeat.

At first no one paid any attention to Old Major, who suddenly rose to his feet and walked to the place where Chris had been working. After a cursory sniff, he jumped down between two of the joists and began to dig. The dirt gave way under his attack, and Jennifer, Julia, and Chris watched in amazement as Old Major dug another four inches deeper. Julia dropped to her knees next to Old Major and began clawing the earth with her hands.

As Old Major sniffed the soil once more and then vigorously attacked the earth, the rotting remains of a leather pouch split

Chapter Nineteen — Thanks to Old Major

open. The pouch was stamped *Clark & Gruber & Co's Bank and Mint*. A pile of gold coins was exposed, forever untarnished, bright as they had been a hundred years earlier when Pierre Prideaux was alive and held them in his hands.

Julia could not contain her excitement, and she danced around the room in a frenzy, first kissing Chris, then Old Major, and lastly Jennifer! Old Major added to the turmoil by barking loudly for what seemed like at least five minutes.

The cache appeared to be considerably more than the family's conjecture. Julia remarked that there had been even more gold, for Yvette took her dowry, her own gold, and Pierre's gift to Andre with her when she traveled to New Bordeaux.

"It's *truly* incredible!" she added. "Aside from what the old mule carried, Pierre must have been an unusually powerful man to have borne so much weight when he and Yvette walked out of Clear Creek Canyon."

Later that evening, just before dark, Chris and Julia were sitting on August's veranda eating a dish of Mrs. Janning's homemade ice cream. Julia scraped the last drop from her bowl and licked the back of her spoon.

"We'll have a terrific homecoming for Matt."

Chris nodded. "Thanks to Old Major! It's a good thing dogs love to dig. Jennifer was right. He is someone's ghost, all right — but he isn't Custer's."

Julia's curiosity was aroused and she asked, "Why not Custer?"

"Custer was temperamental," said Chris. "Old Major isn't at all like Custer."

Chris didn't enlighten Julia further and after cogitating for several minutes she laughed.

"Of course! Old Major is Andre's ghost! Who else walked with a limp and was easygoing. I'm quite sure Andre knew all about the gold!"

Chris finished the last of his ice cream. "Are we going to recover the rest of Pierre's gold?"

"The rest? What are you talking about?"

Chris reached for Julia's empty ice cream bowl and stacked it with his on the table beside his chair.

"Pierre didn't take his entire fortune with him when he left Clear Creek Canyon. I reckon there's a good share of it still in the place where he buried Madeline."

Julia was astounded. "How strange! None of my relatives ever thought to check out Pierre's claim. It didn't occur to me, either. In her journal Yvette didn't mention the gold Pierre was forced to abandon. I wonder if it's still there."

Chris considered the possibility. "Mr. Atkinson might have been the shrewd one and looked for that gold instead of joining his partners who were following Pierre. Thinking the gold had to be somewhere near the claim, Atkinson might have found it."

"I doubt it," said Julia. "After all, Mr. Dumler failed to discover Pierre's cache, and Mr. Dumler had a big advantage over Mr. Atkinson. Mr. Dumler was with Pierre constantly and was always asking questions about the gold. Also, Dumler was able to watch Pierre's movements. Pierre must have given Anton Dumler the slip every time he went to the mine.

"And the mine holds more than Pierre's gold; it's Madeline's grave. Do you think Pierre would want us to disturb the place where he buried Madeline? I would feel like I was robbing the dead!"

Chris didn't agree with Julia.

"I think perhaps Pierre would agree to it. After all, he had worked harder at prospecting than I can imagine. He would want his efforts to count for something. I would take Madeline three dozen red roses in his name. I suspect he loved her more than his life."

Julia thought a moment. "Perhaps someday we'll look for the rest of Pierre's gold, but not soon. The claim was recorded and Yvette said the mine was on the north face of the canyon. Nature changes the terrain, but maybe we could find the location. Who

Chapter Nineteen — Thanks to Old Major

knows? Let's keep it to ourselves. There's no need to stir up a hornet's nest. Gold does strange things to people!"

Julia reached into her pocket and pulled out a Pikes Peak gold coin.

"I wonder what these are worth to collectors."

Chris took Julia's coin and flipped it into the air, watching the disk as it turned.

"Sooner or later you'll have a fortune Julia, even after the government takes a cut!"

"*We'll* have a fortune," she said firmly. "The gift to Matt will be from both of us. Our folks and Jennifer deserve something, too. And let's not forget Old Major! If there is anything left, let's put it in a fund for college."

Chris's and Julia's world was almost perfect. They held hands and listened to the humming of the cicadas in the hackberry tree and answers from the Osage orange trees along the road.

"I wish everyone could share the peace of a summer night in Kansas," said Chris in a low voice.

It was hard for either of them to visualize what was still happening in Vietnam.

Chapter Twenty

Facing the Vietnam War

July 19-22, 1967

THE FOLLOWING THREE days were uneventful.
On Saturday, at five-thirty in the morning it was still dark as Julia sat up in her bed. She stretched, then threw the covers to one side as she put her feet on the floor and felt for her slippers, at the same time reaching for her robe. For a moment, she wondered why she was awake so early. Then she remembered. She was meeting Chris at five-forty-five. She had been puzzled when he had insisted they take Honey and Batese and ride to their favorite rock ledge west of Hays. They had never ridden at such an early hour.

Julia pulled on her jeans and a T-shirt, then in the kitchen gulped down a glass of milk. After she had brushed her hair and

Chapter Twenty — Facing the Vietnam War

her teeth, she picked up a pad of paper to leave a note for Jennifer telling her where she had gone.

Twenty-five minutes later, when Julia reached August's barn, Julia found that Chris had already saddled Honey and Batese and tied their reins to the corral rail. They mounted their horses and rode west at a canter.

Soon Honey and Batese were climbing the rocky slope to the ledge overlooking Fort Hays. A cool breeze was stirring the buffalo grass in the pasture below the bluff. Dawn was spreading a diffused light across the landscape.

When they arrived at the top of the hill, Chris unsaddled the horses. As usual, he arranged the saddles and blankets on the ground, leaving a space between them.

Chris appeared to Julia as if he had something on his mind, and after a long silence, he finally spoke. "The United States isn't winning the Vietnam War, and sooner or later, probably within a year, I'll have to fight. By now — at least in this county — even married men are being drafted."

Julia visualized what the war had done to Matt. "I'll never be able to stand it, watching you experience what Matt had to endure!"

Chris would not foresee pity for himself. "If I can take what the world has become, so can you. Your strength is one of the reasons why I love you. You don't realize how strong you are."

For the first time Julia knew — finally — that Chris loved her!

But Chris wasn't only thinking about Julia. He was considering the problems he was facing due to the Vietnam War.

"I don't think President Johnson is likely to win popular support for the war. Even so, General Westmoreland is asking for more troops to be sent to Vietnam and Johnson is supporting him. My guess is Johnson will have a tough time winning another term in the White House. And if he does manage to get elected again, I don't see an end to U.S. involvement. No one, not even Congress, tells President Johnson what to do. If Johnson loses the election, his successor, whoever that might be, will either have to fight to win, or wind the war down gradually. And any way I cut it, I can't avoid Vietnam."

Julia struggled to keep her composure. "It just isn't fair."

"Fairness has nothing to do with this problem," Chris answered. "One thing I know for sure . . . I have to live with myself. I'll take my chances, like Matt did.

"Meanwhile, I've made up my mind about something. Will you let me spend whatever time I have left here with you? Can we go steady, and someday get married? Maybe we're just kids, but somehow I feel older."

Julia was overwhelmed by his questions and could only whisper a breathless, "*Yes!*"

"Then I have this for you. . . ."

Chris reached into his pocket and pulled out a piece of white linen. Wrapped inside the cloth was a gold ring, delicately made, mounted with a blue stone. Chris offered the ring to Julia.

"It's a sapphire. It belonged to my grandmother."

Thinking back to all they had just gone through, and remembering Yvette's diary, Julia recalled the pearl ring that Andre had given to Yvette, the ring that had been his mother's. Julia smiled to herself. The sapphire ring size was small, and Julia watched while Chris slipped it on the little finger of her left hand.

"If I could have my way, we'd get married now," Chris announced. "In the South, teenagers marry and sometimes have two children by the time they're our age. But my mother won't buy that argument, I'm sure. . . . She seems to have forgotten that she was barely eighteen when she married my dad!" Chris reached for Julia's hand.

"I can wait for marriage if you can," she told him. "Besides, I like to live one day at a time. Let's enjoy our last year of high school together."

Julia looked at her ring and thought of the promises it represented. Chris thought of the unpredictable months ahead.

"If we're lucky, and if the war is resolved soon, we can get on with our lives," he added. "But, frankly, I'm not counting on it. My feeling is, it could drag on for a long time.

Chapter Twenty — Facing the Vietnam War

"No matter though — for our marriage to be legal, I'd have to convince my mother to sign a consent at the courthouse. By law, girls can marry without parental consent when they're eighteen. I'll have to wait until I'm twenty-one. I'm pretty sure Mom would reject the idea of anything before that.

"But I figure the best time to approach her will be in the spring. Ten months isn't too long for us to wait; it's less than a year. We'll be out of school, and by that time the Army will be staring me in the face. I'll be old enough to fight a war, so she won't be able to insist I'm too young to be married!"

Chris and Julia talked for hours, making plans for the future. When everything was settled, they saddled their horses and rode home, as Julia offered a silent prayer for peace.

Chapter Twenty-One

Home from the War

August 12, 1967

IT WAS SATURDAY, and by chance both Julia and Chris had the day off. Julia had cut short their usual ride, for today Matt was coming home. They had agreed that the family would greet Matt first, alone; Chris did not want to intrude at that initial welcoming.

At five o'clock that afternoon Julia stationed herself near the picture window in her living room. She was intent upon the traffic along Chetola Road, for the station wagon bringing Matt and her father home was due to arrive at any minute. Mr. Simmons was almost never late.

Two days earlier Julia's father had gone to Denver to get Matt, who was a patient at Fitzsimmons Veterans Hospital

Chapter Twenty-One — Home from the War

where he had been assigned soon after his arrival in Hawaii. He had been in rehabilitation, but because he was now an outpatient, he was allowed to go home. Later on, he would return to the hospital to be fitted with a prosthesis.

Julia could hear the sound of pans clattering in the kitchen. Mrs. Simmons was cooking Matt's favorite meal, her own mother's recipe for pot roast. The odors made Julia's mouth water in anticipation.

The minutes dragged by, and Julia stepped outside onto the front porch. Overhead a large flock of Canada geese were calling to each other, on their way to a reservoir. She idly watched them, then shaded her eyes with one hand and studied the formation.

"That's odd," she murmured aloud. *What is a lone snow goose doing in a skein of Canada geese? I've never seen a snow goose around here at this time of the year . . . and certainly not flying with Canadians!* She concluded that maybe it was a good omen.

In the distance Julia caught sight of a familiar vehicle. "They're coming!" she shouted.

Mrs. Simmons hurried from the kitchen. She wiped her hands on her apron then quickly untied its strings, removed the apron, and tossed it aside before she opened the front door.

Julia and her mother could hear the crunch of the car's wheels as Mr. Simmons turned off Chetola Road and began the short drive to the house. When the car was parked along the front sidewalk, Julia and her mother could see Matt, sitting in the front seat looking straight ahead.

Mr. Simmons turned off the car's ignition, and when the engine died, he got out and walked past the front bumper to Matt's side and opened the door. Then he reached into the back seat and retrieved a pair of wooden crutches.

Julia heard the intake of her mother's breath and suddenly she found herself battling a flood of tears. She won her internal struggle and followed behind her mother as Mrs. Simmons hurried down the sidewalk to greet her son. Her extended arms embraced Matt as she cheerfully exclaimed, "We *missed* you, Matt! It's so good to have you home!"

"Hi, Mom," was all Matt said, as he kissed his mother on her cheek. He smiled at Julia, who was waiting her turn to say "Hello."

The four of them made their way up the sidewalk and then up the front steps to the porch.

"You can sit down here and have a nice visit! I must finish my cooking and set the table. I'll call you when supper's ready," Mrs. Simmons added, as she hurried into the house.

Julia sat in one of the wicker chairs and watched her brother as he lowered himself into the porch swing. Mr. Simmons chose a chair where he could see his son's face. His own face revealed the burden of his sorrow.

No one spoke, and Julia sat quietly for several minutes. She thought Matt looked tired. He had a scar above his left ear and he had lost a lot of weight. But it was a relief to her that in most other ways it seemed as if he hadn't changed. Julia's eyes moved down Matt's neat uniform and came to rest on the flap of cloth that had been pinned up out of the way.

He must have been watching her.

"It's not the end of the world, Sis. I'm home, and that's all that matters to me right now. Someday I'll ride Ginger again. Just you wait and see!"

The flood of tears that Julia had conquered only minutes earlier burst forth.

"Come here," Matt said comfortingly, and he moved over on the porch swing, then put his arm around Julia's shoulders.

"You can cry, but only this once. I'm not the same person I was when I left home. I've experienced things I never want to talk about, but I consider myself lucky to be sitting here with you and Dad!"

Just then Mrs. Simmons announced that supper was ready and, like always, told them to "Go wash up!" Julia dried her eyes and forced herself to smile. She gave Matt a kiss on his cheek and told him not to worry about her; she would be OK.

The pot roast was a success. Matt ate until even his father was in awe of his "holding" capacity. And Matt still had room for his

Chapter Twenty-One — Home from the War

mother's cherry pie, topped with vanilla ice cream. By the time everyone had finished eating, they were laughing and chatting together as if nothing had changed.

Mr. Simmons leaned back in his chair. "Two of your friends would like to say hello, Matt. Do you feel up to it?"

"I guess so," Matt replied. "Is Chris at home?"

"As a matter of fact, there's a party for you at Fort Hays in about an hour! It's just Chris and Jennifer. Hope you don't mind on your first night." Mr. Simmons stood up and began to help his wife clear away the dishes. Julia put the uneaten food in containers and placed them in the refrigerator.

When the Simmons' family drove up to the Tourist Information Center, at first Matt thought no one else was there. The door was locked, and it was dark inside. He failed to pick up the undercurrent of excitement in Julia's voice.

"The party is in the blockhouse!" she told him.

Matt was somewhat surprised, for the blockhouse was an unused building and had not been restored. It looked the same as it did in 1867 when Custer was at Fort Hays. But Matt said nothing, and moved along behind his family as they made their way to the octagon-shaped building. As they passed the maintenance tool shed, Julia called to Old Major who came bounding out, ready for whatever was afoot.

When Matt entered the blockhouse, he saw that the room was filled with bright gold balloons. A table with a gold tablecloth had been placed along the west wall. Plates were stacked with bright gold cookies, and a punch bowl was filled with lemonade. Matt made no comment, but he wondered why so much gold had been used to decorate the room.

Jennifer and Chris hurried forward to welcome Matt, and from the shadows in a far corner of the room, a tall young girl with long blonde hair stepped into the light. At first, Matt didn't see her. He was greeting Chris and Jennifer. Then he glanced in her direction and for a moment seemed expressionless, until a huge smile illuminated his face. "Elly!" Matt's crutch dropped from under his left arm as he circled Elly's waist and then buried his face in her neck. After a long moment, Chris reached down and retrieved Matt's crutch.

Everyone began talking, and soon they all had a chance to visit with Matt. After he had caught up with almost everything that had happened while he was gone and during a lull in the conversation, Jennifer asked the group to be quiet.

"We have a surprise for you, Matt," said Jennifer in a voice that could hardly contain her excitement.

At that moment Julia and Old Major stepped to the center of the room.

"Actually, Old Major is the one with the surprise," Julia added. "Why don't you call to him and see what he has?"

Matt was not well acquainted with Old Major. "Come here, boy!" he coaxed. "Show me what you've got!"

Old Major was sitting next to Julia. In his mouth he held a large, yellow leather pouch. As Matt urged Old Major to bring it to him, Old Major began wagging his tail. Soon his hindquarters were sweeping back and forth on the rough pine floor.

"What's in that pouch? . . . Bring it here, boy."

Old Major, still wagging his tail, rose to his feet and walked toward Matt. He dropped the pouch with a thud at Matt's feet and sat down. He gave his gift a final thorough sniffing before he looked up at Matt.

Elly reached down, picked up the pouch, then handed it to Matt, "This is for you!"

When Matt pulled open the thongs and turned the pouch upside down, a stream of Pikes Peak gold coins cascaded to the floor. He was almost speechless, as he finally realized what he had. "You found Pierre's gold!"

When the babble of explanations ceased, Julia was able to recount the events that had at last revealed the location of the cache. She explained Yvette's obscure riddle, which now made perfect sense.

Chapter Twenty-One — Home from the War

Later that night, long after the party was over, when Julia was in bed, she gave thanks for Matt's return from Vietnam, and for the insight that had enabled her to solve the riddle of the lost gold. She was supremely happy, for Matt would have the horse ranch he had longed for all his life. And when she thought about the future and her life with Chris, she was determined to put the specter of Vietnam out of her mind. *Scarlett O'Hara had the right slant on things*, Julia said to herself as she fell asleep . . .

"*Tomorrow is another day!*"

Selected Reading

Custer and the West

Father Blaine Burkey. *Custer, Come at Once*. Hays, KS: Society of Friends of Historic Fort Hays, 1991.

Elizabeth Bacon Custer, with Introduction by Jane R. Stewart. *General Custer in Kansas and Texas*. The Western Frontier Library, Volumes I, II, III. Norman: University of Oklahoma Press, 1971.

Everett Newson Dick. *Sod House Frontier*. Lincoln: University of Nebraska Press, 1954.

Lyle W. Dorsett and Michael McCarthy. *The Queen City: A History of Denver*. Volume I, Western Urban History Series. Boulder, CO: Pruett Publishing Company, 1977-1986.

Mary Einsel. *Kansas — The Priceless Prairie*. Coldwater, KS, 1976.

Fred S. Kaufman. *Custer Passed Our Way*. Aberdeen, SD: North Plains Press, 1971.

Leslie Linville and Bertha Linville. *Up the Smoky Hill Trail in 1867 with an Ox Drawn Wagon Train*. Osborne, KS: Osborne Publishing Company, 1983.

Thomas B. Marquis, with Introduction by Joseph Medicine Crow. *Keep the Last Bullet for Yourself*. New York: Two Continents Publishing Group, Ltd., 1976.

Leo E. Oliva. *Fort Hays — Keeping Peace on the Plains*. Topeka: Kansas State Historical Society, 1980.

Luther Standing Bear, with Introduction by Richard N. Ellis. *My People, the Sioux*. Lincoln: University of Nebraska Press, 1975.

Robert Wallace. *The Old West — The Miners*. New York: Time-Life Books, 1976.

Vietnam

Huynh Quang Nhuong, with pictures by Vo-Dinh Mai. *The Land I Lost — Adventures of a Boy in Vietnam*. New York: Harper and Row Publishers, 1982.

David K. Wright. *War in Vietnam*, Volumes I-IV. Chicago: Regensteiner Publishing Enterprises, Inc., 1989.